DEWDROPS

DEWDROPS

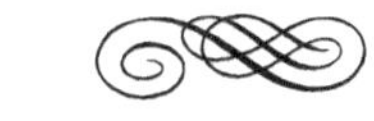

SARAH ELLIOT

Contents

To my parents, as always for giving me the confidence to keep on going

Awwwwwwwoooooooooooooooooo!

One

Prologue – Red and White Ribbons

Rain always fascinated Tristan. Most cubs hated the rain when they were first born, choosing to shy away from it as it was just a constant wetness that fell from the sky and they were unable to process it. But even when Tristan was a newborn cub, his parents said that he adored to just sit and watch the raindrops fall down from the sky. Either that or he would trace the little patterns against the window with his snout. Many adults called him cute, saying that he probably had a natural affinity to water, meaning that he would probably turn out to be an omega one day, but Tristan and his parents did not really pay attention to the classic stereotypes.

Water for an omega, earth for the betas and fire for the alphas. This was the general rule when it came to underlying elemental affinities and the more traditional wolf packs would rigidly follow it to the letter. Tristan, along with his mother and father, were more of the modern ideology that a certain affinity didn't necessarily align with what the cub would present as. They were just happy to allow the young cub to grow and present naturally, inherently becoming who they were meant to be rather than being forced into a specific role.

Tristan was carefree and a spirited character, happy to go exploring and adventuring whenever the opportunity presented itself. He was always looking to be involved in something that would undoubtedly cause mayhem for someone, somewhere down the line. He never had malicious intentions, as he had good morals and knew to stop when some others did not. Even when the weather would keep him in the house, his parents knew that there was a reasonable chance that they would discover that all of the towels from the airing cupboard had disappeared to make a fort. Or perhaps that there would be hundreds of building blocks all arranged to build a city in the living room. Maybe the bathroom would have been turned into a science lab? There always were any number of crazy adventures that Tristan could have become involved in.

He kept a record of all his adventures, in what he thought was grown-up handwriting, in a large book which he had discovered in the attic that held nothing but blank pages and the words 'Account' in faded typography on the cover. It was missing the U and one of the C's however so it was his 'Acont' book. He had never bothered to fill in the missing letters of the word, despite being able to clearly see them and owning several gold pens he could use to correct them. He hid the book under his bed so that he could work on it in secret at night under the covers with a torch. Of course, his parents knew all about the book but saw no harm in Tristan keeping it as they could see it was a good way for the little wolf to practice his words, spelling, sentence structure and everything else that he would need to do when he got to the Whispering Academy.

Tristan was really looking forward to those days, even though they were so far away in his nine-year-old mind, but he had promised that he would strive hard and become the best student in the school. Then he'd meet the ideal mate and they'd graduate together, and everything would just be like a dream. Like his current obsession of 'High Paw Musical' where everyone got together with perfect mates. It made everything seem so much better and brighter. No one had bothered to quite explain to the youngster that that wasn't how it was in the real world, but they could see no harm in it. Besides, pretty much all of the other children in Tristan's class had watched the film as well and it served as a good playground game. The craze would probably die out within the next month or so anyway. At least that's what Tristan's mother prayed for. If she had to hear another rendition of 'Summer Puppy Love' she was going to take something rather heavy and throw it at someone. Namely whoever had introduced Tristan to the film in the first place or even better the producers of the movie who should have known better than this.

However, today was a soggy, wet Saturday afternoon. Tristan was indulging in his favourite childhood pastime of simply watching the rain fall. Whilst most others would be as far away from the windows as possible, he was idly colouring. Distracted by the rain, he did not notice or care that he was filling something in a bright shade of orange that really shouldn't have been that colour. His five-year-old cousin Viola was also colouring underneath a blanket fort which they had made earlier out of a clothes horse and the covers from their beds. She was apparently colouring in a princess coach from her colouring book but had decided that its primary colours were going to be orange and blue and no one was going to stop her. Plus, it was adorable to watch the biscotti-eared girl concentrating so hard with her little tongue poking out to the side, so the elder cub allowed her to be.

Tristan was curled up in one of the large bay windows, tracing the patterns of the raindrops with his fingers whilst he cuddled an old, much-faded, forest-scene blanket to his small body. A flash of lightning caused him to glance up, and he started counting the seconds in his head to see how far away the storm was. One tail wag, two tail wag, three. The lightning came down brightly and made the cub smile widely. Though for just a second he was confused as the lightning seemed to be going on for longer than it needed and was moving. But upon closer inspection, it turned out to be a van going along the street. It was moving way too fast though, but Tristan knew he couldn't call out to it so opted to just ignore it.

Suddenly another clap of thunder was heard overhead and the little wolf instinctively felt like letting out a howl, but before he could Violet let out a whine of fright which caused Tristan to lose interest in the van completely.

"It's okay Vi," Tristan said, turning to face his little cousin who had gone a pale shade of white at the first sound of the thunder, causing her little, biscotti-coloured ears to flatten in worry and dismay. "It's just Old Farmer Jack rolling potatoes down the stairs! Nothing to worry about."

Unfortunately for Tristan his funny, little story did not sit well with Viola. When the next clap of thunder sounded like it was directly over their house, the little, five-year-old girl let out a shriek of fear and raced away to find her mum so that she could wail, cry and genuinely be the child that she was. Tristan wasn't overly worried about that though. He knew very well that Viola did not like thunderstorms, just as most cubs were fearful of them. He just tended to cope better with them. Letting out a sigh, Tristan reached up to scratch at his own chocolate-black ears, determined to get a tangle out of them that had developed over the last day or so.

He blamed it on the rough boys who he had been trying to keep away from the girls in the park. Tristan could play with all the cubs that he wanted because he would constantly switch his moods around to match with his playmates. If someone wanted to rough and tumble, then he would oblige them for hours. If someone wanted to sit in human form and play tea parties with their dolls, then he would join in with a happy smile. He'd play on the swings, rush down the slide, or draw pictures in the sand. He would climb trees, make up adventure stories, and go around fixing everyone's booboos with a little plaster pack filled with 'Space Buddiez' characters. It was extremely cute and he got so many comments about how he would be amazing when he grew up, no matter what he presented as. There were still two years left to go before his pre-presentation at ten which would start him down the path to becoming either a beta, an omega or an alpha. His father had a playful betting ring going to guess the secondary gender of his child, a common occurrence throughout many of the local packs. These were never taken too seriously as most of the bets were based on who would be eventually hosting the presentation party. The elder wolves generally kept it a secret from the youngsters, only letting them in on the secret once they had fully presented somewhere between the ages of sixteen and eighteen.

The best odds at the moment was that Tristan would pre-present as a beta, but his mother had always said that she was carrying a level-headed alpha. Tristan was unique in his family as his coat was a luscious chocolate-black that was flecked with small, white, fluffy bits that made people think of stars. In wolf form, he appeared to be almost like a patch of nighttime sky which had fallen to the ground and taken on the form of the most adorable cub in the world (according to his mother). As a human he was of average height for his age with messy, black hair tipped naturally with white that had to be tamed not only with a brush but with a wide assortment of styling products. He had deep, dark blue eyes that gave him a wise look and he was just a happy cub who did not worry too much about life in general. He went with the flow, threw on whatever clothes he felt were appropriate for the day and just had fun. Today he had chosen an old, 3/4-length shirt and a pair of dungarees with the knees nearly worn through. The outfit had seemed appropriate as he planned on going out to play with his friends but then it had started raining.

Something that people realised about Tristan as they came to know him, was that he had an extremely protective side that many referred to as his 'alpha' coming out to play. The few times that the alpha side had come out it had been extremely frightening to those who had witnessed it, though nobody ever spoke of what happened aloud. Some of Tristan's friends had deserted him after he had expressed this alpha side to a boy who was picking on Viola in the playground one time. Tristan had just shrugged it off with a nonchalance which betrayed his young age. "I didn't do anything to them, if they're that scared then they're being silly and should think about where they stand in the world."

His father had talked long and hard to Tristan about those words, wanting to make sure that his son had not picked up some strange concept of how an alpha should be. Eventually he came away from the conversation seeming satisfied and with a smile on his face. He told his wife that, whilst their son would indeed be very unorthodox, he was most certainly an alpha who had pride, knew his place in the pack and what would be expected of him one day. The odds had doubled on Tristan presenting as an alpha, but it was still an open game.

Since that incident Tristan had kept only a select group of friends, but he did not seem to be troubled by it. Even on a day like today, with thunder rolling, lightning streaking through the sky and sheets of rain crashing down, Tristan did not feel troubled about not being able to go outside. He could just enjoy watching the storm.

He could never explain why he enjoyed watching this weather, it just always felt so freeing to the little, nine-year-old cub. Almost as if the water could bring something to him that no other element could. Letting out a sigh as his warm breath had misted up the window, Tristan tutted in annoyance and leaned across to rub at the glass with the sleeve of his shirt to clear it.

"Naughty breath, blocking my view." He spoke aloud to himself, not really caring if anyone heard him or not. "You know I like the rain, why did you do that?"

Having finished his little task, Tristan smiled and glanced out of the window just as a long, forked streak of lightning crashed down into the street in front of his house. Everything was illuminated for several seconds with flashes of white, blue and that strange colour he could never quite describe before it all disappeared. Though as Tristan blinked his eyes to dispel the strange spots of colour that were now temporarily burned into his vision, he saw something that had not been in the street before the rain had started.

For a second he thought he was just seeing things, until a second flash of lightning illuminated the large, black van that had just slammed its doors before it began to speed off into the dark streets that were awash with the rainwater. Tristan felt an odd sort of pull in his gut, something telling him that he had to go outside, right this second and that he couldn't delay.

Tristan naturally followed this instinct, pausing only long enough to pull on a pair of yellow wellington boots and a green raincoat which fit snugly around his head as he remembered to flatten his ears. The tip of his tail would dangle down into the water on the ground but that was a normal occurrence. Instinct made Tristan also pick up a secondary raincoat, this one a light blue with yellow ducks on it. He was pretty sure it belonged to one of his cousin's friends because Viola certainly would not entertain ducks on her raincoat. Though he didn't dwell too much on that thought as he reached up to grab the spare key from the little hook nearby, used it to open the door, replaced the key and then headed out into the driveway at the front of the house. He did put the snib on automatically so that he could avoid getting locked out.

He didn't know why this would be important, but it was something that his instinct taught him to do, so he just followed it. There was no need to question anything at this age, questions were for grown-ups anyway, and Tristan certainly wasn't a grown-up.

The temperature outside was far colder than Tristan had expected it to be, but he did not let that thought phase him as he was still so certain that there was something else that was far more important than being cold. The rain continued to lash down, bringing with it the smell of wet earth that tickled his nose in the most delightful way. As he passed the car at the end of the driveway and headed towards the small road that connected the estate, the horrible scent of burnt gingerbread, mixed with vomit and blood filled the air. There was a high-pitched wailing sound as well, but the storm was drowning that out, so the cub was not entirely sure if it was connected to the stench or not. The assault on his senses was overpowering, causing the young wolf to stagger back a few steps. Part of him wanted to just turn and run to go grab his parents to let them know something was wrong out here.

Tristan did not do that, as all his instincts were screaming at him to go and find the source of the rotten smell and offer comfort to it. There was no time to think, no time to waste, Tristan just had to reach whoever was that distressed and help them. It wasn't just the most important thing right now; it was the only thing in his life in that singular moment. Nothing was going to stop him from going and giving what help he could to whoever was hurt

Tristan's yellow, welly-clad foot stepped into what should have been a fairly deep but clear puddle, but instead disturbed a ribbon of red that swirled almost uselessly back and forth in the water as though it was not meant to be there. Childish curiosity made Tristan lean down, carefully dipping his fingers into the red ribbon to see if it was attached to something only to find that his fingers came away with red stains on them and the rest of the ribbon remained in the water. It took him a few seconds to process the fact that this was blood in the rain and out of shock and childish nature, he initially looked up to see if there were any more ribbons of red coming down from the sky. Then his ears pricked ever so slightly in his hood as a tiny whimper of pain started up. Even though Tristan was only nine, he recognized that sound instinctively, and he ran straight towards it.

It was a high-pitched sound, like the ones his mother made when she was in distress and it always made Tristan want to immediately go and comfort her. This one was heartbreaking and unmistakably the sound of an omega in pain. He hadn't heard the actual call too many times, at least not in this context, but Tristan's natural instincts had taken over with the need to protect the injured omega. Any wolf who heard that pitiful sound would want nothing more than to rush to the omega in question and help them. It was an instinctual element that categorized the relationship between all wolves regardless of secondary gender.

Tristan had no qualms in continuing down towards the end of his street, now oblivious to the rain as the tiny whimper started to get higher in pitch. It was so lonely, so upset, so terrified and Tristan wanted nothing more than to bundle whoever was making that noise up into his arms and protect them forever. It was probably one of the reasons why, when he rounded the corner, a yell of sheer panic, disbelief and horror escaped from his lips.

Lying on the kerb was a child, no older or younger than Tristan, who did not even look real. Their skin was pale and lacerated with wounds that dripped more ribbons of red than Tristan had seen in his life. The other boy also sported a crop of dirty blond hair that was messy and stuck to a sweaty, shivering forehead. He also had the largest champagne-white tail and set of ears that Tristan had ever recalled seeing on one so young. They looked to be almost adult-like, but were covered in muck and grime. The child was devoid of clothing, allowing Tristan the chance to briefly notice that there was a huge concentration of red ribbons around the lower regions of the boy – a male omega Tristan figured as the distressed wail could only be coming from him – that looked as though it had been roughly cut open and then sewed back up again by the most inexperienced person in the entire world.

However, what startled Tristan more was the fact that the tiny omega suddenly looked up at him with the most stunning emerald-green eyes that were laced with pain, terror, and the want for someone to just hold him and never ever let go. For a second, they flashed a stunning ocean-blue. Tristan was unaware that just momentarily his own eyes shone a deep, passionate red before fading back to their usual blue colour. The pair stared at each other, the rain lashing down as if the world was waiting with bated breath for the next moment to occur.

Tristan moved first, hurrying to the boy's side and pulling the spare coat with the ducks out across the injured omega's shoulders and wrapped it around his injured form. It was slightly easier as the omega was clutching his arms to his chest. A stuttering breath left both of them and the omega lowered his head as tears started to hiccup out of him.

Tristan wrapped both arms around the small-framed youngster in a hug, knowing that they were the best thing when someone was upset and feeling the need to embrace this injured stranger. He even placed the smallest of pecks onto the top of his ears which was purely instinctual once again. "Shh, it's okay. I'll call for my mummy really quick and then we'll get you someplace safe. Okay?"

The boy did not answer, instead sobbing harshly and tried to claw at his chest which instinctively Tristan tried to stop. "No, no... Don't do that. You're already hurt and that will make it... What?"

Tristan's eyes had naturally been drawn to the spot where the terrified youngster was attempting to claw at and to his surprise and horror he saw two small bundles of very wet fluff that were attempting to suckle on the slightly extended nipples that should not have been on a boy of this age. Tristan was stunned into silence before the white-eared boy let out a sobbing squeak, stretching his hand away from himself as if to reach for something.

Tristan turned just in time to see a third, almost invisible, ball of black fluff skirting the edge of the nearest drain. Moving quickly, Tristan leapt the ten-foot distance to the bundle which had snagged itself on a stick and quickly pulled it into his hands. Stepping back from the gushing waters, he protectively cradled the rescued fluff. He blinked away the rain that was dripping into his eyes and found himself staring at an impossibly small, white, sightless wolf cub who must have literally been only a few hours old as it snuffled at his fingers trying to get some milk.

A numbness took hold of Tristan for a few very long seconds, before he suddenly became aware of a large umbrella opening just above his head. He looked up, seeing a brightly coloured pattern of flowers and happy words written on the inside and an old grandmother with redwood-coloured ears, tail and a smile that assured that everything was going to be all right. "Let's get the little one back to his mama, yeah?" Her voice was soft, yet ancient and powerful and she guided Tristan back. Tristan recognised her as Grandma Zuzu, the old lady who ran the bakery in town that he liked to visit. He didn't think to question why she was here, just allowed himself to be guided by her. Gently Zuzu placed a hand on top of the injured boy, looking so sad for him before she nodded. "I'll fetch someone to help both you boys out. You're good."

The next second there came the frantic sound of Tristan's mother shouting from the doorway upon realising her son was missing. Blinking, Tristan looked down to find himself kneeling right next to the boy who had three cubs desperately trying to get some milk out of his body though even Tristan could tell that the boy wasn't able to provide any. By rights, he shouldn't even be able to have cubs and something terrible had to have happened to his fragile body.

Tristan blinked again, leaning down to press a warm hand on the side of the boy's face before gulping. "I'll help you. I'll make you strong again. Just trust in me, I won't hurt you."

Raising his head up, Tristan howled loud and clear for his mother, telling her exactly where he was. She couldn't help but let out a shriek of fear when she came around the corner to find the horrendous sight which Tristan had been dealing with for the past few minutes. It did not take long for his parents to have the white-eared boy carefully picked up from the road and moved into the house, along with the cubs who refused naturally to be separated from their mother. The boy was placed next to the fire in the main living room, more towels and blankets being brought to help cover and warm him and the cubs. The cubs were also offered some extra comfort items like plushies and pillows. The boy was offered some food but refused to even look at the adults, crying openly now.

Tristan's father took charge of ringing for an ambulance and the police, his eyes showing clear signs of distress and anger over this whole situation. Tristan did not blame him in the slightest. In fact, for the first time in a long while, the nine-year-old felt like he wasn't much help at all because the grownups were fluttering around and appeared to be just dealing with whatever needed to be done.

Tristan did the only thing that he could think to do, which was to sit quietly next to the unnamed boy who had fallen into a light doze from exhaustion and very carefully combed out the knots from his hair and ears. It was the least he could do so that they wouldn't get all clumped up and become painful. The adults let him do this, seeing as it appeared to keep the injured boy calm.

Suddenly the mysterious boy's eyes snapped open, a frightened squeal escaping from his lips, but Tristan just rested his hand upon his head and stroked through the locks. "Shh, it's okay, my little one, I'm here."

The emerald-green eyes swivelled up in fright towards the sound of the voice, the mewling of the pups going completely unnoticed. Tristan doubted that if the boy knew what was going on with his body at the moment. He found himself fascinated by those eyes. They were so deep and dark, and they reminded Tristan of the fields that he liked to play in during the summer.

"Who... Where?" the boy asked, his voice so small, and raggedly broken with coughs that Tristan felt compelled to fetch him a drink and helped him to take some careful sips. There was a basket of soft cookies as well, which Tristan noted were iced in beautiful pastel colours but couldn't place where they had even come from. He grabbed one, broke off a tiny piece and offered it to the boy who hesitated.

"You're safe," Tristan repeated, aware that his mother was approaching. "Wherever you were before, you're not there now. You're here, with me, with my mother, father, and baby cousin Viola." He offered the soft biscuit once again and the boy took the bite so delicately it was a marvel.

The boy blinked again. "Who are you?"

"Tristan," he replied instantly, smiling as he picked up the slight accent in the boy's voice, almost as if he wasn't from Silverhill. "I'm Tristan. What's your name?"

The boy blinked, seeming to look blank before suddenly letting out a yell and slashing his arm downwards towards the puppies who were still trying to drink from him. Thankfully Tristan's mother was close enough to stop him and gently shook her head. "Don't push them, little one. They're just trying to..."

The boy's attention had finally landed on the puppies below him and a heart-breaking cry escaped from his lips as he began to babble incoherently. Tristan could not catch most of the words, it was all a mixed jumble of panic that was to be expected from someone so young. Someone who should not have to be a mother to three ailing cubs who were only trying to survive. Tristan was quick to resume his previous petting, hoping that it would calm the boy down. To everyone's relief it seemed to work though the boy still struggled with his breathing and large, fat tears were rolling down his cheeks.

Tristan gently shuffled his position so that he was lying behind the boy, lying close to him so that he could continue to pet the rough hair and ears as well as hopefully stop him from lashing out at the pups. "You have really nice hair, you know?" He spoke softly, hoping to distract the boy.

This only caused more tears to flow. "No... not... dirty... filthy... wrong... so wrong..."

Tristan's mother let out a sound of distress, mouthing the word 'abuse' to his father who was still on the phone. The alpha nodded clearly in response, shaking with rage and anger for the youngster who was laying on his floor.

Tristan however did not notice, instead focusing on the boy. "No... You're not. They're not."

"Am..." the boy hiccupped back. "Allowed... led on... my fault, all my fault."

"No!" Tristan spoke sharply with a whole lot more conviction to his tone than before. "No. Whatever this is, no. You're just a kid! If a big, mean adult did this to you then they're wrong. Not you. Not these little ones either. You've done nothing wrong."

The boy shook his head, hiccupping as a fresh set of tears started to come out of his eyes as he tried once again to smack the babies away from his body. He could feel their little mouths trying desperately to get whatever nutrients out of him that they could but already he knew that he had nothing to give. His body wasn't prepared for this, wasn't able to cope and he would have preferred it if those precious little dots of light which had just about kept him going in the darkness had not been brought into this world. He knew that he couldn't look after them. He knew that his body held none of the omega traits that were needed to look after cubs and that it would be better if they were gone. He couldn't feed them, couldn't look after them or protect them from the monster in the dark who would just take them away to do horrible things to them. Or worse, just kill them right in front of him.

Above all, the boy just didn't want to look at them. Didn't want to feel that blossoming feeling in his heart, that instinctual nature to protect, to guide, to love them. His precious little babies, the ones that would bring him smiles no matter what happened throughout the years. The ones who would give him a family of his own. The lie that he told himself to somehow survive the nightmare that had become his life because he knew that no alpha would take him on. Certainly not after he had allowed this to happen to him. He was tainted, used, disgusting and didn't deserve a chance at happiness. He didn't want to look at his babies because he didn't want to become attached to them. He didn't want to hold them for a moment longer because if he did then he would never let go and he'd just end up alone, forgotten and another one for the heap.

It was better to reject them. Better to make sure they were taken away from him and given to someone who could look after them. Make sure they grew up knowing happiness and having everything they could ever want and more. That way the pain wouldn't be as harsh, wouldn't linger too long and finally he would be free.

"Off!" He began to chant, not entirely sure when he had started to say that word or why it hurt so much to say it, but he had to do something! He had to get those precious little bundles away from him. They had to be taken somewhere safe. "Off... get them off... please... please... take them..."

"Little one." The female omega from before spoke, her hands soft on his face making him flinch. "They need you right now."

The emerald-green eyes opened, hopelessness and despair flooding them. "I'll kill them. I can't... my body... they're hurting... I don't want... ah!" A pained scream burst from his lips as Tristan's mother looked down to see that one of the cubs had bitten through one of the sensitive teats in its quest for the non-existent milk. It was just causing more blood to flow out of the already bruised and battered body.

There was a frantic sort of panic for a few minutes as Tristan's mother and aunt tried to remove the squealing cubs from the boy. That proved to be easier said than done, however, as even though he had said to take him away some of his natural instincts were kicking in and he tried to fight to keep the cubs at his side. He even bit down harshly on a hand that was just trying to keep his face away from the cubs. He was sure he had bitten hard enough to draw blood and leave a permanent mark but was surprised when no one chided him for it. The voices around him just spoke calmly and with reassurance that the boy honestly found surreal.

It was at some point during this mess of cries, scratches and wails that Tristan learnt the boy's name was in fact Andrew and when the final cub was removed from its mother to be bundled up safely in a warm towel and taken to be fed, Tristan very carefully resumed his position lying behind the fragile boy. Softly, he began petting his ears again, being very careful to not startle him. For a moment it seemed to work until Andrew suddenly lunged for his cubs. As Tristan tried to pull him back, Andrew found himself biting down hard, finding his teeth firmly lodged in Tristan's right hand. It did hurt a little bit, but a strange sort of calm overtook the pair, and then they settled down together.

After a while Andrew released the hand he had taken into his mouth and licked it clean in apology, which caused Tristan to happily nuzzle at the neck of the omega, quite unaware that it was near the scent glands and where an alpha would usually place a mating mark.

After several minutes of this, Tristan found himself singing softly, one of the songs from 'High Paw Musical' coming straight to his mind.

"You are my starlight, the one I need tonight, the one who I will always cherish and love no matter what happens from this moment on..."

Andrew let out a shuddering breath. "You shouldn't say that to me..."

"Why not?" Tristan spoke quietly, aware that there were people talking but he was more focused on the broken, little omega in his arms.

"Because..." Andrew started, hiccupping again, "I'm useless."

"No, you're not." Tristan said the words slowly, nuzzling slightly at the side of the boy's neck.

"You're someone who's been through something terrible, but you'll make it through all that is to come too."

A slightly disbelieving look came from a reflective surface near to where the pair were lying and Tristan couldn't help but smile at Andrew's expression, finding it slightly adorable even if his whole world had been rocked violently. "Because I'm here. I'll be your guardian and make sure that no one ever hurts you ever again."

Andrew was quiet for a few seconds, before he slowly shook his head. "No one can make that promise."

"Well, I can, and I will!" Tristan declared with a fierce determination in his words again.

"You're too innocent for this world." Andrew spoke quietly in a voice that seemed far too mature and grown-up. The statement was filled with so many emotions that Tristan did not completely understand. All he knew was that he wasn't going to give up.

"Who else is going to protect you, Andy?" Tristan replied, deciding that he liked the fit of the shorter name and he was determined to call him it. Even if he got a confused scowl for his troubles. "I mean, you're a long way from home, right? You'll need someone to protect you and I'll do that for you."

A very tired sigh escaped from Andrew, though it was laced with a tiny amount of fondness. He hiccupped a sob and said, "You won't be able to protect me forever."

Tristan smiled. "It doesn't have to be forever, though, does it? I'll protect you until you smile again. How does that sound?"

Andrew was quiet for a long while and Tristan thought that he had gone to sleep. He carefully shifted upright to glance down at the boy to see if he was right. Only to find that Andrew was wide awake, staring at the wall opposite him with a vacant look in his eyes. "Until I smile again..." He spoke in a tiny whisper. "Tristan guards me... though it'll never come."

With that Andrew's eyes slipped closed and a heavy-sounding breath escaped him. Suddenly panic began to swell in the nine-year-old Tristan's heart. He reached forward, shaking Andrew by the shoulder and was terrified to the point of screaming when there was no response.

Medics came rushing in, moving Tristan away from the boy on the carpet as they began their frantic work and Tristan could only scream helplessly at them as he desperately tried to reach out for the boy. He did not understand why it hurt so much, the mere concept of mates was foreign to him at this stage in his life, but Tristan knew instinctively that if Andrew died then his own life would no longer be worth living.

He screamed, cried, and acted up terribly until the moment when Andrew suddenly started to breathe properly again and his heartbeat became steady. Tristan passed out into a deep slumber after that, scaring his mother witless. However, he would wake up in her arms later that evening, knowing that Andrew was in good hands despite not being able to see him. He didn't try to explain this to his parents, as they already had a look in their eye which said that they knew what was going on, but he didn't question it.

He was too young to understand, but he vowed that once he did, then he would make sure that he kept his promise to Andrew. There was nothing that could possibly stop him from doing that.

Two

Heading Home

Watching the countryside flashing by the window as the train rushed smoothly along the tracks, Tristan found himself blinking in surprise as familiarity set in. He knew the hills, trees and small town buildings that were coming into view. The air, even though filtered through the vents above his head, started to smell familiar with tinges of the old sugar cane crops on the far side of town. There was also that heavy, earthy smell that always lingered around that had the wolf in him itching to leap out and start running. It had been five years since he had left but it was nice to see that there were so many things that were still here. Of course there would be changes, but he'd have the joy of finding them out with his beloved omega, Andrew.

The town of Silverhill was a community with a shopping district, parks, entertainment districts and school system but unlike the city it didn't have the towering skyscrapers and busy streets. Here the homes were still dug out of the hillside, modernised for convenience but with large, rolling gardens for the cubs to play in. Trees lined every street to provide shelter and fruits in the summer and fond memories in the winter. There were flowers everywhere. Small, wild, feline cat-sith and canine coin-sith ran about, some with collars, others without. Their wings tinkled harmoniously with the sounds of bells and whistles. A few birds sang songs, whilst a selkie played with water nymphs in a babbling river.

Tristan smiled to himself. He took a deep breath of pure joy at the notion that he would soon be back in the lands of his birth. He allowed himself to indulge in memories as he took a long gulp of the sweet rhubarb tea that he had purchased from the cart earlier, letting his black ears and tail relax just a little bit further.

This was the country where he was born, where he had grown up and experienced virtually all of his firsts. His first few tentative steps into the world. His first discovery of mud and the mess it could make. The first time he had experienced rain and had come to love it. The first time he had made friends, learnt to laugh and started his education. This was the place that above all else would always be his home. When given the opportunity to return to it after years of being in the city Tristan had jumped at the chance. Not because he didn't like the city, far from it! It was a place that he adored because of the possibilities and the ever-changing nature of it. There were many things to see and do in the city. Just so many shops, places of interest and restaurants that dealt in all sorts of different kinds of food from all around the world. There seemed to be an endless selection of different opportunities that made it feel like a never-ending dream.

Of course, there were many bad things about being in the city. The pollution was terrible and resulted in many wolves constantly having to wear face masks to prevent themselves from getting sick. There was also a lot of crime. Tristan had been lucky to avoid getting mugged or set upon by the local gangs that lingered around a lot of street corners. He had known some people who had been caught out and the results were not pretty. Generally Tristan pushed those thoughts to the side. He had dealt with enough depressing cases in his short career as a lawyer in training and it was not something that he wanted to dwell on. Instead he focused on the happier aspects of his life, on the studying that had gotten him noticed, not just by his professors, but by many different high-class organisations who had tried to recruit him for various different posts. However, none of them had seemed quite right and Tristan had politely declined them all.

That was until KVZU offered him a position in their legal department with a bursary generous enough to allow him to take a gap year with only minimal employment. KVZU were a legal firm who dealt with crimes where omegas' rights were being abused. They were primarily concerned with forced matings, abusive relationships and the transition of traditional packs to a more modern ideology. They also dealt with the darker cases and did not turn anyone away. They also fought for the rights of betas and alphas equally, as they knew that terrible things could happen to anyone of any sub gender. The archaic idea that alphas were the leaders, betas the middle ground and omegas the lowest of the low who could do nothing but hold a pup was an outdated mentality that needed to be pushed firmly into the past.

Tristan had always dreamt of getting involved with the company ever since the incident twelve years ago. Now that they had practically offered him a job with a funded gap year and a firm reason to travel back home, he was getting to live his dream. It felt almost a little too surreal, like this was all some fairy tale that would eventually become unravelled. He raised his right hand up to the window to bring himself back to reality. This world wasn't all sunshine, rainbows and peace. There were dark wolves out there. Monsters who would toy with someone's innocence and then destroy it when it provided them no more entertainment. Tristan gently rolled his fingers over the mark on his hand. He recalled the terrified reaction of a tiny omega trying to fight off instincts he couldn't understand. He still had the will to protect and look after three innocent lives, despite trying to push them away because he couldn't physically look after them.

Tristan had never once complained about the bite mark, or queried why it had remained distinctively on his skin. By all medical accounts, it should have disappeared after only a few days. Tristan's parents had been worried about it and concerned for what it might mean. They were uneasy about a whole bunch of other adult things which he had not understood very well at the time. Once he reached the age where the subject of mates and claiming came very hurriedly into their sex education classes, however, his understanding finally came about. Though strangely Tristan was not disturbed by the fact that he had already been marked as Andrew's mate. The truth was that when he had gone out in the rain to answer that poor omega's desperate call, he had already known instinctively that they were meant to be together.

Tristan had always kept contact with Andrew after that day, visiting him at every opportunity until he was reunited with his family. Even then, every day after school and before his homework, Tristan would go to Andrew's house to check up on the omega. He gave him hugs and comfort and shared with him anything and everything that he could. The pair shared toys, clothes, books, stories about their day, even if most of the time it was just Tristan talking about what he had done in school. He'd also bring over sweets and other treats, and soft things that the omega seemed to like receiving the most. Andrew would place them in his nest on the bed and try his hardest to let Tristan into it. He never found the nerve to do it. It had taken a while for Tristan to even be allowed into the bedroom where the nest was built, as Andrew was a little skittish. However, after the first few days Andrew would always be waiting on the doorstep for Tristan so he could give him a hug and receive one in return.

The only real issue came from Daniel, Andrew's older brother, who had become very protective of

his little brother and quite frequently tried to make Tristan leave. He refused to allow Tristan in if their mother wasn't home and would watch the pair like a hawk constantly, growing visibly frustrated if the other boy stayed longer than Daniel thought he should be allowed. One day, Daniel got home after Tristan arrived. Having already had a long and terrible day at school, he had lost his temper and tried to attack Tristan. It had resulted in a huge physical fight between the two, with Daniel desperately trying to get to his little brother whereas Tristan was trying to prevent Daniel from hurting Andrew. It was a mess and no adults were around to stop the fight for the longest time.

It was only stopped when a teary Andrew tried to break up the fight and had been accidentally smacked in the side of the face, causing what would later become a small, white scar on his eyebrow. Both of the boys fighting had frozen in fear at the wail that had come out of him but it was broken a split second later when Tristan literally threw himself into the line of fire and pulled Andrew into a hug. Gently he had cooed at the boy, petted his hair and whispered apologies into his beautiful champagne-white ears until Andrew had calmed down and stopped crying. Daniel had felt so incredibly guilty that he had very nearly left, until his younger brother caught him by the hand and made him join in the hug. It had been a strange day, which only became more obvious when they had to explain what had happened to their parents when they got home an hour later. Ever since that day Daniel had been a big bother to Tristan as well, seemingly intent on making sure that he was the perfect alpha for Andrew.

They still fought from time to time, but mainly it was a play-fight for practice, that saw neither of them really hurt. There was the odd scratch or bruise but nothing that had Andrew running out to them ever again. He'd sit on the sidelines and watch, calling out if he thought things were getting just a little too rough, but otherwise remained safely out of the way. Of course, most of the time, Tristan was more than willing to play less rambunctious games with Andrew, ensuring that he had fun as well and cooing over the pictures that the omega would draw. They looked funny to Tristan, usually showing some kind of fantasy scenery or creatures. There were occasionally ones that the omega would hide from view. Tristan would later come to realise they were of family and the future that Andrew was going to have with him.

Once or twice Tristan found that Andrew had made some cards for his cubs, with shaky handwriting and wonky pictures, but he had never sent them out. Andrew struggled with the mention of cubs at the best of times and even though the three little boys lived with Tristan's aunt and uncle, he never went to see them. A horror-filled look would cross Andrew's face whenever cubs were mentioned, so Tristan had made sure to never say a word. One year he managed to sneak the cards out from the omega's hidden box and sent them to his aunt and uncle because he hoped that one day they would be able to reunite.

The trio had spent many a happy summer together, eagerly anticipating the newest release of the 'High Paw Musical'. It was their favourite movie, even though Daniel said that he was only going to see it under sufferance. It seemed like those happy summers would go on forever, until the day when Tristan had to tell both Daniel and Andrew that he was heading to the city. His parents were moving there and there was no way for him to stay.

Daniel had been quite vocal about it, saying that it wasn't right. Andrew, bless his soul, just stood up from where he had been sitting, wrapped his arms tightly around Tristan's neck and whispered quietly to him, "Come home one day. Please?"

Andrew had pulled back at that point, clearly trying not to burst into a fresh flood of tears. Tristan had then stepped forward, pulled the slightly younger boy into a hug and placed a kiss upon his temple. He had promised that he would indeed return to Andrew's side and that he would keep in contact every single day to tell Andrew everything about the city. He told Andrew that he'd send gifts, postcards and letters or whatever the young omega wanted him to send. Andrew had hiccupped tears throughout the whole ordeal but never let go of his unpresented alpha.

When they had finally parted, some hours later, neither boy had any tears left in them. For the first time that Tristan could remember, Andrew had gently smiled and his heart had practically burst at the sight. It was just a shy, little smile. One that was filled with a gentle happiness and Tristan had sworn to himself on that day that he would always strive to keep giving Andrew reasons to smile like that every day.

Letting out a sigh, Tristan turned his attention away from the rolling scenery to the blue piece of paper that had a cute little rendition of Canine Pup – a character from another childhood favourite, 'Space Buddiez' – in the corner. He wondered if he really needed to finish the letter or not. The alpha had kept his promise, writing every single day to the young omega as well as sending back postcards and pictures. He would also send little toys that he got out of capsule machines that he thought Andrew would most appreciate, as well as a whole bunch of other items on top of it all. It was rare that he got a reply from Andrew, but he understood that writing wasn't the youngster's strong point. He treasured those letters and hand-drawn pictures that he received in reply.

Generally, the pictures hadn't improved in quality over time. They were sort of lopsided and looked very much like a child had drawn them. Half the time he couldn't actually tell what they were supposed to be, but there was something so endearing about them that Tristan had come to love them. He had even framed his favourites and put them on his wall at the Whispering Academy. He got a lot of crazy comments from his friends about them but he refused to take them down and after a while everyone came to appreciate them in some form or other. He looked down at the paper once again and wondered if it was worth finishing the letter. Surely Andrew would be waiting for him to step off the train so they could reunite?

Actually, now that he thought about it, Tristan didn't really know much about what Andrew was doing these days. The omega was very quiet in his letters, only sending back short ones but he seemed to be doing at least a little better. He wrote about attending therapy, getting a job somewhere (though he kept the details vague) as well as some of his studies, but all other details were left out. His letters always contained the phrase 'I miss you, please come home' that made the alpha want to drop everything and return straight to his omega. Now he was here and it was a little bit nerve-wracking.

Particularly because, over the last couple of months, Tristan had started to believe that he was not the most desirable of alphas. For one thing, he was shorter than most, frequently getting mistaken for a beta (or even in some cases an omega) because his height did not really give the impression he was strong and dependable. He was known to have a calm nature, was very inquisitive and sought intelligence rather than strength. He had been told that there was something to his smooth, clear face; dark blue eyes; and curly, warm brown hair, which had been dyed from its natural black. Whatever it was, it just did not make him seem to be an alpha upon first glance. His ears and tail were still the same dark chocolate colour that they had been ever since he was a kid and it was not unusual to find someone cooing over them and petting him. It was sometimes awkward, but Tristan usually felt it would be rude to interrupt, and so was often inclined to let them pet him.

This was particularly true if Chester got a chance to pet his ears. The big beta with the gummy smile and perpetually happy, virus-like personality would spend hours just petting him which went from calm and relaxing to extremely awkward within the space of ten minutes. Mainly because Chester would not stop petting him, even after it was clear that he should probably stop. There again no one could rightfully explain Chester because by all accounts he should be an alpha with his impressive height, easy-going charm and all-round likeability. Yet he wasn't. Tristan suspected at one point that he may be an omega in disguise but this was thwarted when at a party a fight had broken out between two omegas and another beta as to which one of them was actually dating the giant until they realized that they were all being played. Tristan had rapidly left that situation.

When Chester had complained at him later for ditching him and pulled the whole 'bros before hoes' business with him, Tristan had just calmly replied with, "You made your bed, so you sleep in it." The argument was promptly dropped. Thankfully the situation was resolved though it was clear that Chester was to be avoided at all costs by anyone on campus. That lasted about a month before someone else did something even more silly and became the newest topic of conversation. Chester, however, swore off dating and instead focused on his studies which was definitely the better choice.

Shaking his head, Tristan glanced at the letter and decided that it would be best to just finish it off and put it straight into the post box. He was pretty sure that there was one right next to the station and it would be good to keep up the tradition. Hopefully it would bring a smile to Andrew's lips when he realized that he was receiving a letter posted on the same day that Tristan had returned home. That was of course if Andrew was speaking to him, which was a possibility that somewhat frightened the alpha for a few seconds. His thoughts were then interrupted by a happy blip from his phone. It lit up with an icon of his favourite drawing by the omega, which sort of looked like a big, squishy dragon, to tell him he had a message incoming.

The message was only two words long, but it filled the alpha's heart with so much emotion that he could have exploded into a puddle of happy goo.

To Tristan
"Welcome Home."

It was all that he needed to see.

For a second Tristan debated what to put as a reply before grinning and quickly typing out:

To Andrew <3
"Thank you! I look forward to seeing you soon! <3 <3"

He had been told many times that using emojis was a little bit childish but if anyone did tell him off, Tristan planned to just constantly send emoji messages until they agreed that emojis were a perfectly acceptable form of communication.

Two seconds later came the response of "<3" to the message he had sent. The alpha squealed so loudly that the old grandmother on the opposite side of the carriage had to let out a hearty chuckle. She made a fond comment about the times when she had been in the throes of young love with their own partner all those years ago.

Ah. Young love.

Three

Cubs at Play

There were a series of loud screams from the garden that made Viola look up from preparing the food for the party. It didn't take her long to realise she didn't need to start panicking right away. Kelsey and Fabian were engaged in another game of crazy antics once again, which involved running around the back garden, screaming their heads off and occasionally tackling one another in a sort of dominance game. Being pre-presented omegas, the boys were liable to let off steam in this fashion, but it never really bothered the biscotti-coloured wolf. Games were meant to be played by all, regardless of whether that was playing with dolls, running around with a ball or playfully wrestling each other. All of it was perfectly natural and encouraged by everyone. Sure, it could get loud, but that was cubs in general.

Viola had been the same at that age and even though she was now fully presented, with all the joys of having to deal with being in heat and related issues, she still found that she could just do whatever she wanted and not be bothered by anyone. If she wanted to dress up in pretty skirts and blouses to go shopping with her friends, then she could. If she wanted to have a pair of loose sweat shorts and a ratty, old t-shirt that had been gifted to her by her father and go play football with the local boys, then it was fine. They weren't living in the thrall of the traditional packs, which demanded that young omegas should only behave in one way. Being pretty, subservient and preparing to take up house and home. Sure, Viola wanted a mate, but not just yet. She had her own dreams and plans for what she wanted to do with her life.

There came another scream from the garden and the elder omega glanced up to see that Kelsey had pushed Fabian over and started to play-fight with him. Looking at the pair, Viola let out an amused snort and thought about letting down her light grey hair from its ponytail to make herself appear as fearsome as possible to get the two to behave themselves, but she couldn't really be bothered. It was nice to just watch the rose-white and cupcake-white cubs play-fight. Sure, they had probably wrecked their clothes which meant yet another change, but thankfully the party wasn't for another hour so there was nothing to worry about. Plus, cubs went without clothes most of the time because they couldn't quite control their instincts to change. Viola idly wondered which of the pair had instigated the play-fight but decided it wasn't her issue.

She had a feast to prepare and, while she had made good progress already, there was still lots to be done. The tear and share bread and sausage rolls were in the oven, along with wedges and a selection of chicken, fish, and beef burgers as well as some extra vegetable pasties. A huge bowl sat filled with chicken salad with three optional dressing choices; a big cake was baking in the other oven; the rice cooker was at maximum capacity; and she was in the process of starting on the snack selection. This included crisps, nuts, berries, grapes, a selection of home-wrapped herbs and spices alongside some dried vegetables. There were desserts to do but she already had her little helper working on his section and she wanted to get the snacks on the table and out of the way first before getting the desserts underway.

Vaguely she wondered where Daniel was, as he had promised to turn up to help out, but then realised that he'd probably be making sure that Andrew was doing okay. While she did not know the full details of everything that had gone on, the young omega knew enough to have more patience with her future in-law. He had been mistreated terribly, in ways that no one should have ever had to go through and it was just downright horrific to think that any alpha could do such terrible things. Taking a deep breath, she pushed those thoughts aside as a timer dinged to alert her that the apple tartlets should be done and she quickly moved across to the stove to grab them, with her oven mitts ready to go.

As the warm air hit her, the omega found herself wondering once again if Andrew would gain the courage to come to the party to see his cubs. It would be understandable if he didn't, but it still hurt sometimes. Fabian and Kelsey were past the age where they really should stop asking questions but now their noses were starting to catch scents, they had started to recognise his gingerbread scent that clung to the small packages that Andrew would send them. This would then lead them to asking questions that no one had the answer to. Alban did not seem to be as bothered by such things, on the surface, but it was clear that the three cubs were more than just curious now about their mother and why he did not come to see them.

Especially when his future mate's aunt was raising his cubs as her own. Not that Viola wanted them gone. As far as she was concerned they were her little brothers and anyone who hurt them was going to get bitten. She had always been protective of them and would always be, because they were precious souls and they deserved anything they ever wanted.

Placing the tartlets down on a cooling tray, Viola looked up to the window to see that the pair were still fighting and were now very muddy. Letting out a groan, she reached across to open the window and hollered, "Hoi! You two! Knock it off! I don't have time to give you each a bath!"

Kelsey stopped immediately, his white ears flattening in fright as he particularly disliked being scolded. By contrast Fabian let out a rude sound at Viola before attempting to reengage Kelsey in the play-fight that they had been in before. However, the rose-white cub was having none of it and snapped in irritation towards his brother, which caused the cupcake-white wolf cub to whine loudly in a fake huff and go stomping off.

Viola groaned and threw down her oven mitts. "I don't have time to deal with this."

"Want a hand?" asked a deep, soothing voice from behind her. Viola turned with a relieved sigh to see Daniel standing next to a happily working Alban, absently petting the cub to let him know that he was there.

Alban, the last of the cubs in Viola's vision, had decided that he did not feel up to playing in the back garden with his brothers and had offered to help his big sister with cooking. He liked to be helpful just as much as he liked to play, though he preferred to stay inside most of the time. If anyone asked, he would say it was just easier to concentrate when there was less background noise as he didn't have the ability to hear clearly. Alban was diagnosed as moderately deaf but over the last year or so it had started to slip towards severely. However, he did not seem to be too distraught by this, as everyone in the family used sign language. His friends at school had also learnt Makaton from an early age. Daniel knew it was best to let Alban know that he was in the room when he arrived, so he didn't get startled. Plus, it gave him an excuse to pet the cub which was always a good thing in his book.

The cub looked up with a bright grin, his blue eyes sparkling happily in contrast to his naturally soft, white hair. His sable-black ears flicked back and forth in time with Daniel's hand. "Uncle Daniel!"

Daniel smiled and nuzzled the young cub affectionately, as he always did these days. "Hey sprog! How are you doing?"

He slightly misjudged the level of his hand and poked Alban on the nose, but the cub did not seem to mind and playfully poked him back on the nose in lieu of response.

Viola chuckled. "If you don't plan on getting totally enamoured by our little biscuit decorator then I could use a hand getting Kelsey and Fabian washed up for the second time today."

"Ah, the scoundrels at play?" Daniel asked, ruffling Alban's hair before standing up to allow the cub to go back to his previous task of decorating duck cookies. He frowned for a second, wondering if they were anywhere near Duckimass which was a summer-time festival, but then figured that they were the only cutters available that weren't the yule ones.

The door opened as Kelsey appeared, pouting with tears in his eyes. He was soaked to the bone, his shoulder-length, dark blond hair in horrid little clumps on either side of his face. Small shivers periodically ran through his small frame. "What happened?" Viola demanded immediately, rushing to the aid of the boy who was sniffling away.

"We tried to get rid of the mud," Kelsey managed to stammer out, just before Daniel wrapped the boy in a towel to start drying him off. "Fabian dropped the bucket by accident."

Viola looked furious for a second and turned to glare out at the garden, only to spot said bucket on the floor and a worried, shaking, white cub by the tree. He was just as soaked as Kelsey and had more mud on him than before. She deflated with a sigh. "Oh sweeties, you should have just come in and I would have given you both a bath."

Kelsey blinked and looked meek. "I'm sorry."

"Don't be. It was an accident," Daniel said, blinking when Alban turned up with a very warm-looking bedtime hoody that reached nearly to the cub's knees. It was decorated with Canine Pup cartoons and was very soft to the touch. It only took a few seconds to pull it over Kelsey's head. The change in colour of the blond-haired pup was immediately obvious. "There, that's better. Now why don't you help Alban decorate the biscuits for a few minutes whilst I go fetch Fabian. Then all three of you can have a bath to get ready for the party this afternoon, hmm?"

Alban pouted. "No bath!" he signed.

Kelsey chuckled, "Fabian will just throw bubbles at you till you get in anyway."

For a second the eldest of the cubs seemed to ponder this notion before pulling a face that had Kelsey laughing but grabbing his hand. "Come on, gege. Let's get a head start and find the best bath bombs, huh?" he suggested, addressing Alban with an affectionate term for elder brother.

The notion of bath bombs cheered Alban up immediately and they ran off holding hands. The trio of cubs never really needed to sign to one another in order to communicate. No one could explain it, it was just their way.

Daniel laughed as the pair disappeared before turning his attention back to Viola. She was in the process of loading up the oven with more cooked goods. "You feeding a small army?"

"Have you met our family?" Viola chuckled back, having long ago accepted that she was always going to be teased for making too much, but experience told her that having more was always best. "I bet you I'll have no leftovers even with the extras that I'm going to make today."

"Can you make up a box for Andrew?" Daniel asked gently, hoping that Viola would not make too big of a scene about the situation.

The biscotti-coloured wolf flicked her tail towards him as she finished closing the oven door. "I thought he was going to meet with Tristan at the train station?"

Daniel nodded, scratching at his slate-grey ear out of nervous habit. "He is... but I don't think he'll come here afterwards. Maybe next door but even that's a push now."

Letting out a sigh, Viola mentally checked herself for getting her hopes up. She knew that it would be nothing short of a miracle for Andrew to come to their house when the cubs were around. It was impossible to blame the elder omega, he had been forced to have cubs when he was far too young to even comprehend what that meant for him. Even with the specialist treatment and putting him directly in front of the three cubs that he had birthed would be nothing short of disastrous. Anyone could see that. But there was still a great deal of care and love for the cubs held within his heart. He regularly sent care packages and had been doing so for quite some time. They came with small gifts, like homemade cookies, or school stationery items or even fun books or toys that he had found. The cubs adored them, saying that they came from the Gingerbread Dragon and tried to send their own letters and gifts back. Though whether Andrew got them was something that Daniel kept a secret and would not talk to Viola about.

Plus, on the trio's birthday, a small special present would arrive for them, very plainly spelling out the love that Andrew had for all three of the boys. Despite his worries about not being able to love them the right way.

Viola could only hope that one day he would be ready to face actually speaking with his sons. "He shouldn't be punishing himself like this though," she said softly.

Daniel nodded his head in agreement. "He's trying Viola, he really is but I still don't think he truly understands what happened to him. I mean, I've seen the look in his eyes when he gets pictures and videos from you... He wants to be part of their lives, he really does, but he just can't shake off the feeling of... Well, you know."

Again, nodding in response, Viola gave her elder friend a little shove. "Well hopefully with Tristan's return things will get better, right? Speaking of which, you best go and get that mud monster in before he catches his death of cold."

Saluting playfully, Daniel headed out into the back garden to try and find Fabian. It was a very easy job as the cub was very visible from his position under the apple tree. His cupcake-coloured fur stood out against the rest of his surroundings. The cub looked terrified, almost as if he were about to be punished for getting both him and Kelsey soaked. It made the elder alpha remember a time when he had accidentally turned Andrew blue after trying to clean him. He thought he was using a blue bar of soap, but had managed to mistake it for the dye you use to actually make soap. Thankfully it had only lasted a day, and the photographs were still hung in the hallway because they always brought a little smile to Andrew's face which was something that their mother always encouraged. Cubs were meant to do stupid things, if it came from a good place then there was really no harm done.

"Oh, I wonder why there is a soggy lump of snow hiding out beside the apple tree," Daniel called, hoping that teasing the cub a little would make him become aware that he wasn't in any trouble.

Fabian still ducked back, whimpering in a way that seemed to say: 'I didn't mean to do the bad thing, I'm sorry!' It resonated so solidly with Daniel's being that it was impossible to ignore.

Daniel hunkered down next to the cub. "Oh cubby, you're okay. Nothing bad has happened, you were just trying to help out and it went slightly wrong."

Fabian still whined, clearly worried about being told off and not being allowed to attend the party later. Tristan needed time to bond with the cubs in his own way. They had been so tiny when he last saw them, and it was hoped that if the alpha could form a bond with them then his omega would come around to the idea that he could safely be around them. It was going to be a task and a half, but Daniel was sure that Tristan would bring so many good things back to Andrew's life that it would be worth every last second of waiting.

Daniel shook his head and bent to pick up the cub and hauled him upright. "Let's get you inside and dried off a little. Then you can join your brothers in the biggest bubble bath that I can manage."

That caused Fabian to transform back into his human twelve-year-old body. "Kelsey and Alban are already there?"

"Yep," Daniel said, nodding as he started back down the path. "They're choosing the bath bombs as we speak."

Fabian wriggled a little in excitement. He really loved having a bath with bath bombs in it. Then he hesitated. "Is Viola mad?"

"Nah, she's busy cooking and baking," Daniel replied. "You know that makes her the happiest wolf on the planet."

"I should still say sorry to her," Fabian pouted. "She asked us not to get too dirty."

A quick glance into the kitchen window gave Daniel a smile. "I don't think she's mad, cub. Just concerned. You can quickly say sorry to her though and then we'll head on up to get washed."

Putting the boy down on the ground, the slate-grey wolf smiled proudly for a second and then had to run to the kitchen as Fabian had sweetly hugged his big sister to apologise, but accidentally placed his cold hand on her stomach. This caused her to jump in shock and knock over one of her bowls, causing its contents to spill onto the floor. Viola chased them both out of her kitchen brandishing a large wooden spoon and yelling loudly about what she would do if she caught up to the pair of them. Her words, however, were punctuated with laughter - she couldn't help but see the funny side of it all.

Fabian reached the bathroom and flung himself at his two elder brothers, causing that last bit of chaos before Daniel was able to wrangle all three of them into the bath. There were lots of bubbles and water splashing which meant everything was as it should be. The evening ahead was sure to be interesting, Daniel mused as he made sure the cubs all got clean. He couldn't wait to see how it all played out.

Four

Reunion

A blip on his phone brought Andrew out of his quiet contemplations as he flicked his champagne-white ear towards the sound. Picking the device up from where he had dropped it in an embarrassed panic after sending that last ridiculous emoji message, the omega was surprised to find himself looking at a series of photographs. Not from Tristan but from Daniel with a message just before saying;

> To Andrew:
> **'Cubbies in the tub!'**

The pictures were of Alban, Kelsey and Fabian all in the bath tub that Aunt Paige had installed years ago when they had outgrown the old one. There were lots of brightly coloured bubbles already in the bath as well as a bubble machine churning out its share as well. Fabian was trying to eat all the bubbles from what Andrew could see, whereas Kelsey was mixing up what he hoped was a cocktail of different shampoos. The alternative was that crazy slime hair thing that had been going around the nursery that Andrew worked at. He dreaded to think what state the boys' hair and fur would be in after that. Alban had his bright pink, bonnet-style shower cap on to protect his ears, as getting water in them always made them tingle according to the cub. The idea that Alban suffered from any discomfort, even something as mild as a 'tingle' would send Andrew into a guilty downward spiral. That was until his mother had reminded him that he had told Tristan to go and save Alban the second he noticed the cub was gone from his side, despite being in a terrible situation himself. She had gently told him that it had been his unconditional love that had saved Alban and one day he would be able to accept it but Andrew always denied it.

Deep down he knew the denial was a lie to himself more than anyone else in the world. He did love his cubs and was so thankful that they were growing, happy and clearly so loved. He couldn't quite bring himself to face them yet, but the omega was going to try one day. When they were old enough to understand and could make their own choices.

The final picture was of the trio, wrapped up in warm, fluffy towels with silly, little hooded blankets over the top. Fabian in a Canine Pup one, Kelsey in a Panther Kit one and Alban in a Dusty Rabbit one. Each was squealing joyfully at receiving a new set of 'Space Buddiez' keychains that the omega had sent along with his last package from the Gingerbread Dragon. Immediately his inner omega was dancing around screaming, "Cubs happy, cubs healthy, cubs received toy! Love cubs!" while Andrew tried to take several deep breaths in order to calm himself down. He knew that they'd accept the keychains without question, they were really too cute to not accept but there had been a little touch of doubt in him even though he had been doing this for a while now.

It had been his therapist who suggested that he contact the cubs this way, sending them small care packages filled with toys, stationery, little pieces of sweets or his own baking if he felt like it and just notes to explain. At first Andrew had been resistant, saying that it wasn't right for him to want to build a connection with the three of them after so long. However, after lengthy discussions with his therapist and his mother, he came to the general conclusion that now he was older, he could deal with the trauma of having cubs so young. He doubted that he'd ever be a true mother to them, that ship had probably sunk years ago, but that did not stop him from having a relationship with them. The boys were growing up, all pre-presented as omegas and at that age where no one could stop them if they sought out information on their birth mother.

It had still taken Andrew the better part of three months to build the first package and get it delivered to the trio's home, even though Paige always insisted the door was always open and the kettle would be on instantly. He had been in pieces once it was gone, convinced that the cubs would reject it as it was from a stranger and they weren't supposed to accept anything from strangers. Only to have his nerves completely soothed when Daniel sent him pictures and little video clips of the cubs receiving it and their happy expressions and voices had just melted away his doubts. He'd immediately started on the next box and now sent them regularly every month. Daniel would deliver them in person and take all the pictures and videos to send back to him. He'd also added Andrew to the family photo album where Paige, her husband Paul and Violet uploaded pictures and videos along with Daniel's and slowly he became accustomed to watching his cubs through it. He never let on that it was usually the highlight of his day but Daniel seemed to instinctively get that. Their mother was also added and frequently had lunch dates with Paige, as they had been friends before, but she didn't visit the cubs directly too often as she was still looking after her youngest cub. Always playfully berating the omega when he would try to get her to stop because as far as she was concerned, Andrew needed the looking after until his alpha returned home to take over that duty.

She did meet up with her grandkids, getting them to call her Ayi (a local word for auntie) Timothea and the cubs loved her.

A couple of times they had tried to arrange a meet up between the boys and Andrew, but it had never worked out. Andrew was always conflicted about meeting the cubs in person, too afraid of what he would do to them when they were the innocent parties in all the mess that a monstrous alpha had caused all those years ago. Although he had mostly accepted that none of it had been his fault. His therapist had said that he was actually following his omega instincts, prioritising the cubs' protection over everything else in his life. Andrew had dismissed it even if he secretly agreed that it was exactly what he was doing. He wanted to protect those cubs, to ensure that they never went through anything as horrific as he had been forced through. Though he worried that he'd try to claim them like he had done with Tristan on that night. Not that the alpha had been disturbed or worried, as the bond was only partially created. It was the only reason they had been able to stay apart for so long. Andrew had promised in his letters that they'd court first and ensure that they were meant for each other before making any further commitments.

He had never told Tristan that his pack mark just above his heart had become defined the very night that everything had gone down and he had always been able to see the matching one on the then unpresented alpha's chest. The marks were faint with intention but no commitment though they would fill out perfectly once they were mated. That thought sent way too many neurons in Andrew's brain firing in the wrong direction, so the champagne-white omega instead focused back on the photographs and wondered what he would do if he did ever meet the cubs in person. Smother them to pieces with hugs, kisses and scent them up a storm probably, if he was being truthful with himself. He fondly pushed that thought to the side.

"Just... too... cute," Andrew whispered to himself, once again looking at the photographs and practically curling in on himself to just coo and squee even if he was out in public in the train station of his hometown. A second blip came up, showing yet another photograph but this time of the cubs now all dressed up smart and proper for the party. Kelsey was in a green chequered shirt with a red bow tie, and a red pinafore dress over the top, whilst Fabian had a red chequered shirt with a pair of dark green trousers with braces and a matching bow tie. Alban was in a knee-length, chequered, red and green dress with a pink bow around his left ear.

Without thinking about what he was doing, Andrew quickly typed out a message and pressed send before he could stop himself.

To Daniel:
'Give them all a kiss from me.'

For a second he paused, then shook with disbelief over what he had done before hiding the phone away against his chest, praying that Daniel would understand.

Of course, five seconds later, there came a merry little ping from the phone as Daniel replied with;

To Andrew:
"Yes Mama!"

Deflating a little at the word, Andrew shook his head and locked his phone, glancing back at the tracks where he could see Tristan's parents waiting for him to arrive. Part of his heart knew that he could just go and sit next to the alpha and omega who had always been there whenever things got tough but for some reason today, he just couldn't. There were too many thoughts racing around his head, making him anxious and uneasy, even around people whom he knew would look after him to the ends of the earth. He was just not having the best of days.

Paige had waved to him when she first spotted him, her soft, bouncy curls of fine silver contrasting with her blackberry-coloured ears and tail which wagged happily at the sight of him. She had patted the bench next to her if he wanted to come across, having strategically placed her large, ever-present handbag in the spot next to her after she had ordered Paul to go and get them some hot beverage from the drink kiosk. Paige always seemed to be in tune with Andrew, keeping him in the loop whenever she got the chance but always allowing him to stay at arm's length, if he preferred it. It was clear that Paige wanted Andrew to feel like he was part of the pack, that he was always welcome to attend but she never pushed.

Andrew had waved back but opted to sit alone at the further end of the station because he just couldn't decide how he felt about today. His, or at least what he hoped was his, Tristan was coming back, which was something that he had been looking forward to since the moment the alpha had left. They were going to court one another properly, as fully grown adults and not two kids who were thrown together by circumstances that should have never occurred. It hadn't been the easiest of roads, but in some ways Andrew was grateful to have had the time to find himself through all the madness. Just like there had been times when he hadn't been able to process the fact that Tristan was no longer there. But eventually he had started to push through the pain, confusion and trauma because he needed to be there when Tristan came back into his life. He didn't need to be perfect, that much he knew, but he needed to be able to stand on his own two feet at least a majority of the time.

Today, however, Andrew felt a whole new wave of anxiety trying to eat him up. A pointless, little, lingering fear in his heart that Tristan wouldn't be his Tristan anymore. That the city would have changed him and that he was coming to close the bond between them so that he could move onto a prettier, more sensible omega who wasn't broken and could give him everything that he wanted in a mate. It was his biggest fear, one of the few nightmares that lingered in his sleep.

Scared of losing again; scared of being left alone; scared of having his worst fear confirmed; and that he would be forever just left wallowing in the darkness. Viciously he shook his head, barely able to suppress the thoughts that were lurking there, but trying his hardest. He had to focus on the positives, the fact that Tristan had texted straight back with his funny little emojis and did not question who it was who was texting him. The fact that he had kept his promise of sending him letters and gifts every single day that he was away.

Letting out a sigh, Andrew glanced across at the fields and felt as though a heavy weight was sitting upon his shoulders. What if he had changed too much for Tristan? He was no longer the little boy who could be called 'My little One', as Tristan had affectionately dubbed him. Andrew had grown far taller than anyone had expected and developed strong features that were sharp, yet smoothly sweet when he smiled. He still had dirty blond hair though he opted to wear it slightly longer, and his champagne-white ears and tail were fluffy and so soft to the touch that many people wanted to just pet him for hours on end. His emerald-green eyes were not as prone to shifting about these days and looking for signs of danger constantly. He could hold eye contact without flinching but he still did not quite feel settled into his body somehow.

What if Tristan no longer liked how he looked? Well, he supposed he could change, but he didn't really know how to do that and it felt wrong even if he wasn't fully comfortable in his frame right now.

The chimes of an announcement started, causing Andrew to flick his ears towards the sound to confirm that the train arriving at platform four was indeed the city train which he had been waiting for and it thundered into view with a slight spray of steam that for a moment covered the station. Fear began to grip at Andrew again, because what if Tristan wasn't there? What if he wasn't going to pay even the slightest bit of attention to him and he was just going to be left all alone in the world with no one who would ever help him? It was so tempting to just turn tail and run, to leave the station and leave all the worries behind because maybe he didn't deserve the second chance that he had been longing for.

Maybe this was his punishment. Maybe he deserved to just be on the outside, to see the world through a looking glass and not have to experience the joy and happiness that everyone else got. Maybe he had done something sinful and wrong and he was just disgusting. Maybe all the hope that he had was going to be for naught.

"Andrew?" a voice called quietly from the platform though Andrew did not want to believe that he had heard it. It was just a quiet, little sound that could have been anyone saying a name that wasn't his, and he really needed to run away right now. He needed to get away before he was seen, so that he didn't disappoint Tristan. He knew that he had changed so much and he was sure that Tristan would find him ugly because he was still covered in the filth that had poisoned him so much.

"Andrew!" The voice was closer, though it really shouldn't have been and Andrew felt completely sick now, unaware of the fact that he had curled himself up into a tight ball and was clinging desperately to his hair. There came the sound of running feet, heading straight towards him and the urge to run nearly took hold of him but for a sweet voice calling, "Little one!"

A pair of arms wrapped around Andrew in such a tight, loving hold that the omega was thrown completely off balance for a second. The freshest scent of tea tree oil filled his nose, clearing away all the dark thoughts instantly to make the omega melt into the embrace with an embarrassed whine that was filled with so much confusion and affection that it surprised even him. Andrew felt as though he was out in the wilds, in a fresh forest breathing in the clean air whilst a gentle campfire crackled somewhere nearby. Slowly he opened his eyes, turning to stare up at the alpha and felt his heartbeat quicken as a blush crossed his face.

Tristan was so mature, with beautiful lines and a glimmer to his dark blue eyes that were now more alluring than they had ever been before. They were sparkling with so much happiness and life that for a moment Andrew did not recognise the fact that he was the source of it. He found himself breathless and that was a fraction of a second before he registered the fact that there were lips on his own and he realized that Tristan was kissing him. Actually kissing him, though he had no reason to. Except just maybe...

Andrew suddenly found himself letting go of all of his inhibitions and throwing away all the negative thoughts that had plagued him for far too long. He allowed himself a chance to just exist in this moment. He returned the kiss to Tristan's lips, even though he hadn't a clue as to what he was doing and found his arms were wrapping tightly around Tristan as if to confirm that he was there and wasn't about to disappear as the train pulled forward with another blast of steam coming from its undercarriage.

Tristan pulled back, panting a little in surprise but with the most beautiful smile on his lips before he placed his hands on either side of Andrew's face. "I missed you so much, my little one."

Andrew found himself unable to speak as he broke down into tears, but this time it was out of sheer relief and joy because Tristan was there. Tristan was still his and even though he didn't fully understand how he had marked his mate he was just so thankful that Tristan wasn't going to be leaving him anytime soon. He hugged tightly into Tristan's chest, clinging with all the strength he had and feeling a little shameful for covering the other's shirt in tears but from the happy, rumbling growl that the alpha gave off it was clear he did not mind in the slightest.

Finally, the omega was able to pull back and just look at Tristan, hurriedly wiping away at the tears which still spilled from his green eyes. "I'm sorry..."

"What for?" Tristan replied, moving his fingers across Andrew's face with a tenderness that tugged at his heartstrings.

"I sucked at keeping it in... I just..." Andrew hiccupped again, trying to stop himself from crying but finding his words cut off when Tristan leant across to capture his lips in another kiss.

"Don't worry, I loved all I received and even got teased for having the pictures framed and put on my walls in college." Tristan smiled brightly, laughing at the look of shock that crossed the other's face.

"You did not?" Andrew asked, flushing a bright red. "Oh my goddess, Tristan!"

"What? I thought they were the cutest things ever," Tristan replied, grinning as he pulled the omega back into his chest. "I even brought them home with me in their frames cause they're going up on the wall no matter what you say."

Hiding his face in his hands again, Andrew leaned heavily against Tristan and tried his hardest not to unleash a strangled whine, which had Tristan laughing at him as he lightly rubbed his cheek against Andrew's crown, lightly scenting the omega as his own. "It's okay my love, things are going to be fine. I can't promise you that it'll happen overnight, but I'll be there every single step of the way."

Slowly Andrew pulled back to look at Tristan, his eyes reflecting all sorts of emotions as he took a shuddering breath. "Thank you."

"I made you a promise, didn't I?" Tristan said, gently cupping the side of Andrew's face once again, "And I intend to keep it. We will be a family Andrew."

Lowering his eyes slightly, Andrew let out a sigh, gripping onto Tristan's arm gently. "You... do you... I mean... the cubs... I..."

"I know enough," Tristan said, gently reaching to scratch at Andrew's ear. "I'm not going to blame or judge you because I found you that night and I understand. But we can work on it together, I think that will be for the best. Don't you?"

Nodding again, Andrew latched back onto Tristan and let himself just relax in his presence. Too long he had hidden in his own innermost darkness and it was clear that he would need a beacon to guide him back out of it. Tristan was his beacon.

It was going to be a long road to recovery, one that would take time and patience but with Tristan by his side, Andrew felt as though he could do anything. If this was what having a mate was all about then he was certainly glad that he had claimed Tristan as his all those years ago. This feeling of security was something that he felt he could never let go of now that he had been reminded of how it felt.

A polite cough caught the pair's attention and Paige smiled at them from where she had leaned down to get their attention. "Sorry to interrupt but you will become the web's cutest couple if you don't move quickly."

Sitting near to them was a group of high school students, who were recording all that had happened on their phones with gleeful faces. Clearly they were drama fans who adored seeing the real life versions of true romances occurring and, without meaning to, Andrew and Tristan had become just that.

Andrew blushed as red as a beetroot and stood up hurriedly, almost wishing he could disappear. Judging from the expression on Tristan's face he felt exactly the same. Though a second later, the alpha exclaimed, "Whoa! Andrew! When did you get so tall?"

Blinking, Andrew stared down at Tristan and suddenly realized that his main worry for their relationship had not even crossed his mind. During the course of growing up, Andrew had inherited the height from his mother's side of the family and now stood at six-foot-two whereas Tristan only stood at an average height of five-foot-six. The contrast was surprising but also adorable as Paige cooed at the pair of them which caused more blushing from Andrew.

However, Tristan just chuckled and looped his arms tightly around Andrew's middle. "Well, we're sure going to get some funny looks aren't we, my little one?"

Somehow, hearing those words out of Tristan's mouth settled any remaining worries that Andrew had and a slight smile crossed his lips as he looked away.

Paul chuckled as he finally made his way across to his son and future son-in-law. "Well are we going to stand around here all day, causing a scene or are we going to actually head home? I'm sure that Viola's is going to be livid if the food she's cooked goes to waste."

Tristan grinned. "Oh! Viola's famous cooking! I can't wait to try it." The alpha seemed to pause, realising something quickly which made him squeeze Andrew just a little tighter around his waist. "You are getting a lift home with us right? Not to my home obviously but then..." He paused, quickly racked his brain once again. "Breakfast, tomorrow, at the cat-sith café you like? If it's still there of course."

Andrew shyly nodded. "Yes, it's there. I really shouldn't intrude though."

"Andrew," Tristan said stubbornly, "I'm not having you walk home or get a bus. You're coming home with us and my aunt and uncle won't mind dropping you off."

Paige cooed very loudly which made Tristan blush and playfully swat at his aunt who immediately ran off and the pair merrily chased each other around the car park like they used to do when Tristan was small.

Paul turned his eyes towards Andrew. "You are welcome to the party, you do know that right, Andrew?"

Andrew nodded and swallowed. "Yes. I just... not yet."

"Okay, I'll get lots of photos for you then." Paul smiled, carefully placing his hand on the small of Andrew's back to guide him forward, his big, bushy, maroon-coloured tail whipping back and forth in delight. "Though I'm sure Daniel will already have a pile of them for you."

A slight upturn of the corners of the lips was his reply and together the pair caught up with their mates to get in the car. Andrew was still not sure he could ever be fully at ease around his cubs, but he was sure to start trying because now he had Tristan by his side, there was a new hope in his heart.

Five

Playing Tumbles

If there was one thing that Viola had learnt over the years of helping to raise the cubs, it was that there are three types of alphas. The first type being those who fall firmly into the stereotype of being big, bad wolf alphas. They're more interested in strutting about as though they have the biggest dicks, the best mate and the most precious everything. The ones who spent more time in the office than at home and disregarded everyone; unless there was something that could be gained from beating them or they were in need of satisfying their physical needs. They typically regarded their 'wives' – never mates – as merely someone to produce a worthwhile heir and then a host of pretty sons and daughters to marry off to others like themselves. Thankfully most of those alphas were firmly embedded into the traditional packs out in the countryside and rarely interacted with anyone outside of their own circles.

The second type of alphas were a little more respectable when it came to having mates, as they typically tended to cherish and love their families, but they could be quite demanding and have excessively high expectations. They were generally the type of wolves who got good jobs and worked hard to provide for their families so it was understandable that their stress would leak out in other ways. Most alphas fit into this category out of nothing more than societal demands. They weren't violent most of the time, but they were prone to outbursts. They treated their mates and cubs well, whenever the chance arose and that was the best thing about them.

The third and final type were rare and almost too good to be true in Viola's opinion. They were the ones who strove to keep their mates happy and cared for. They made all the romantic gestures without prompting and never let anyone hurt their mates. Her mother had laughed when she had once stated this theory to her, saying that when she found either her beta or alpha mate then the whole world would open up into a completely different meaning. Viola had rolled her eyes at the notion because she was a modern wolf of the world and knew so much more than her mother did at her age. Paige had smirked at the irony but left her teenage daughter to her whims.

Viola had been worried that Tristan would turn out to be the second type of alpha, one who did a good job of everything but lacked what she called the spark. But as she stared at her elder cousin, who was currently running around an open space of the garden playing chase with Fabian with the biggest smile on his lips, it was clear where he fell in the rankings. Tristan, despite being small, was the third type of alpha without question. He would work hard to provide for his mate, cubs and ensure that any other pack members were treated with just as much care. He already cherished Andrew to the ends of the earth and she would not be surprised if in the next year or so that there would be a blessing from Amarok herself for their mating ceremony. She wasn't that jealous over their pairing, as she knew that they were star-crossed mates, but there was a tiny twinge of envy in her heart. She brushed it aside and finished adding another cake to the already groaning table.

The sound of giggling made her glance across to see that Fabian had managed to tackle Tristan down to the ground and was beaming in victory, even as the larger alpha hoisted the white-eared cub up above him. The pair were covered head to foot in grass stains and it made Viola feel like delivering the pair a dose of sass. Plus it was her prerogative as a younger cousin to tell the elder off when he was making a mess. "Tristan! I just gave him a bath not a couple of hours ago! Look at the state of you two."

Tristan laughed at the expression that Viola was pulling, hoisting Fabian into the air again to make the youngster squeal happily. "Oh, stop complaining, Vi. Cubs are supposed to be covered in mud and dirt. It's perfectly natural."

Viola shook her head again, "You won't be saying that when you're the one trying to give him a bath later on."

"Hey, how come I have to give him a bath?" Tristan responded playfully, tugging Fabian down into a bear hug to ruffle his hair. "I'm the one who just got home!"

"Yeah, and you've got off lightly with the fun and games, you little twerp. It's your turn to play daddy," Daniel said as he passed by, giving a cheeky smirk with an accompanying flick of his slate-grey ears and tail in a playful challenge that immediately made Tristan break out in a grin. Within seconds the two (supposedly grown-up) alphas were tumbling on the grass like two cubs and making an absolute embarrassment of themselves, but no one really cared.

It was hard to care about anything too much considering that it was a nice sunny evening, there was plenty of food available and the pleasant atmosphere in the garden that made everyone inclined to just enjoy themselves. Sure, Tristan was being a little on the silly side, but wolves liked to play with one another regardless of their age. It helped create bonds and gave them all a good chance to figure out the hierarchy in family packs. Plus Tristan and Daniel had been play-fighting since they were small, so it was really nothing out of the ordinary.

It all stemmed from instinct and the pair having to prove to their inner wolves that Tristan was more than capable of protecting Andrew from any threats. Daniel's wolf sometimes felt a little encroached on as Andrew was his omega baby brother who had been ripped away from him, hurt in the most brutal of ways and he had utterly failed to protect him. Even if he had a huge scar on his back from where he had fought as hard as his then ten-year-old body would allow him. Whilst it was rarely talked about, Daniel had nearly died protecting his brother and it still haunted him that he had lost and taken nearly six months to recover from the beatings that he had been given. So naturally when Andrew was returned, Daniel had been extremely protective of him, even when it came to the prospective future mate. Thankfully they had resolved most of their issues, but the pair still liked to throw themselves into mock fights just to prove what had long since passed between them.

Everyone just found it amusing and knew to step out of the way once the pair started, the scuffles would resolve themselves in the end. Though Viola did call them a bunch of silly names before heading off to refill the drinks table, despite Paige telling her to relax and enjoy herself.

After around ten minutes, the two grown-up alphas tired of their game, mainly because Tristan kept pinning Daniel firmly to the ground and refusing to let him up until Fabian decided to help his uncle by tickling Tristan's foot. This caused Tristan to jump up with laughter, which allowed Daniel to spring up and pin Tristan down with a smirk. Thankfully Fabian decided that he couldn't just allow this to happen so had then tickled Daniel behind his knee and kept going back and forth until the two alphas decided that they had had enough and pinned

Fabian down to blow raspberries onto his tummy and 'pin' him down with hugs.

The cub had squealed merrily before wriggling away from the pair and running off which allowed the alphas to catch their breath and giggle with one another. As well as prod some fun as they always would.

"Finally able to beat me, eh? Little twerp." Daniel grinned, shaking his head slightly to get rid of the blades of grass that had clung to his hair.

"I could always beat you Daniel, you just had too much pride to admit it." Tristan grinned casually back, dusting himself down and looking around. "Oh, I take it Andrew isn't coming?" he asked quietly, a little disappointed, not wanting to disturb the happiness of the others around them.

Andrew had ridden in the car with him as had been requested, their clasped hands never leaving one another as they remained together in the back seat. But when they had reached the familiar street where the omega lived, Andrew had asked to be dropped off and Tristan's uncle obliged, telling him to be safe. Tristan had tried to go with Andrew, but the tall omega had just shaken his head, lightly kissed Tristan's lips and said that he would see him later.

Daniel shifted a little on his feet before letting out a sigh, "He's not ready for this kind of thing yet. Plus, with the cubs... don't worry about it tonight. Just have fun and make sure you bond with all three of them."

Tristan nodded. "I intend to, as much as I can. Do you know where Kelsey and Alban are?"

"Probably in the playhouse down the bottom of the garden, next to the apple tree." Daniel smiled, pointing to the area. "Though you may want to take some treats across cause they're both quite shy, little things."

Nodding his head, Tristan glanced towards the table that was over-flowing with food, and then towards Fabian who was also eyeing the table but with a calculated look as if he wanted something specific that wasn't there. The cub let out a pout and then shrugged before rushing off towards a toy box that was just inside the folding doors to the living room to start digging through it for something. He seemed to be the most active out of the three that the alpha had met, and he figured that it would be probably better to just leave him alone to his own devices for a little bit.

Besides, Viola had just come back from the kitchen with several large jugs of juice so Tristan rushed over to help her bring the heavy jugs to the table and set them down. "How do I best approach Kelsey and Alban?" the alpha asked gently. "Or what's their favourite sweet treat? Fabian was looking at the table before, but I don't think I've seen either of them eat anything yet."

Blinking in surprise, Viola paused as she thought about the question before making a silent 'follow me' signal and heading back into the kitchen. Once there, the omega used a foot stool to reach a tin on one of the higher shelves that was kept very neat and clean from what Tristan could see. The tin was shaped like a cute, white, fluffy coin-sith pup wrapped in a large multicoloured scarf with golden fairy wings. Tristan immediately recognised it.

It had been prominently displayed in the window of everyone's favourite bakery shop, Zuzu's, which was run by a lovely, old grandmother with smiling crescent eyes, redwood fur on her large expressive ears and tail. She always instilled a joyous peace in anyone who walked into her store. She knew each and every person by name and could provide exactly the baked goods you needed at that specific moment. It was almost like she had a second sense to know when you were coming in and what you needed. Although whether it was through intuition or magic no one could say. Tristan had only paused in consideration once when he found a similar place in the city, but had forgotten his concerns once he had been presented with a piece of rose flower cake that was almost identical to his aunt's and hadn't questioned anything further.

The tin that had been on display had enthralled Andrew so much that Tristan had spent two months saving up all his allowance to buy it for the omega and presented it to him at Duckimass. Andrew had been so overjoyed with the gift that he'd hugged it tightly, then been more surprised to discover that inside it held a selection of biscuits in eight different flavours of cream cookies with strawberry, green tea, raspberry, chocolate, blueberry, lemon, lavender, and honey as well as a small, thin, leather-bound recipe book for the cookies in question.

The trio of Andrew, Tristan and Daniel had spent a merry Duckimass by the pond sampling all the different flavours and choosing their favourites, whilst wearing bright yellow duck hats and matching wellington boots.

Tristan let out a noise upon seeing the tin and made grabby hands towards it, which confused Viola for a second before she rolled her eyes and handed it across. "Before you ask, yes it was Andrew's idea to use that tin for the biscuits and he insisted that the cubs keep it. They wanted it kept special so that's why it stays up the top there, out of the way."

"Does he use the recipe book that came with it?" Tristan asked, all starry eyed at the very notion that his omega was using the tin he'd given him to send precious biscuits to his cubs. It was doing things to his heart and mind that were definitely not too becoming but he didn't care.

Viola snorted. "Of course, you really think that Andrew would use store bought biscuits for his cubs? They're actually really good too."

The alpha fell to his knees as his heart burst with the utmost joy and love for his sweet omega. Even though Andrew had not actively met his cubs, he was still providing for them with his own hands. Still caring for them even though he feared that he would hurt them in some way. Tristan knew he was biased towards the other, because he knew him so well even if they had been apart for years but it still warmed his heart to know that the omega hadn't lost everything that night. Even if it was just unconscious and instinctual, Andrew still loved his boys and Tristan had already fallen for them even with just his brief interaction with Fabian.

He sent a prayer of thanks and love to Amarok, as well as to Andrew because the omega deserved to know that he had done so well and his alpha was proud of him. Even if it were over a distance, if a bond was strong enough mates could sometimes sense the feelings of each other. It wasn't deliberate, but by the confused tremors that came back through the bond that he had with Andrew, Tristan could tell the omega had picked up on his pride. The alpha let out a very happy, and love-sick-sounding grumble of a very contented wolf.

Viola made a disgusted face at him, though her eyes were shining with joy before she playfully batted his arm with a long-suffering sigh. "Honestly! You two are going to be the most gross couple on the entire planet if you keep on going like this."

"I don't know what you mean, Vi." Tristan grinned, practically singing the words.

"Who's being gross and freaking you out now, Vi?" A new voice joined the conversation as Nathan wandered into the kitchen with a wide smile, his hair fluffed up just ever so perfectly and his eyes alight with good-natured humour. He had been friends with Viola for years, though quite what he was always remained a bit of a mystery. They called him a Frey as his appearance was constantly different and he never had any markings of a wolf. If asked outright, he would just completely change the subject.

His wide eyes wandered from a distraught looking Viola to Tristan and within a second, his face also took on a disgusted expression. "Ugh, goddess, so they are," he stated before suddenly leaping forward to tackle hug Tristan with a squeal. "But so, so cute though! I just want to put them into a box together and make them kiss! I'm totally going to be the one organising your mating ceremony and I don't care what the old beanstalk says, he's having one regardless and..."

"Whoa, hey calm down Nathan," Tristan replied, petting the others head gently. "We've got quite a way to go before all of that and right now I'm on a mission."

Nathan immediately switched his personality back to a diva with a sassy expression that was naturally highlighted by his thick eyeliner. No one was quite sure if Nathan just opted to switch between these two personalities, or if he had some kind of condition that triggered him into doing so but after a time everyone came to just accept that this was how Nathan was. "You are seriously not going to try and woo him with biscuits are you? That would be so corny and downright cheesy that I'm going to throw up if you even attempt it."

"I'm actually trying to connect with my future cubs," Tristan shot back at the other with a grin. "Vi is helping me by getting them some treats. I'm just so happy that they're in the same tin that I bought for Andrew years ago."

"Oh," Nathan blinked and made a small, circular 'O' shape with his mouth. "Right, okay... still gross but yeah... err... oh Leroy! Let me help you with that."

Viola's eyes opened in fright as Nathan took off at a sharp speed towards Leroy who appeared to be moving something and hurriedly the smaller omega leapt down off the stool to go rushing after the pair. Not before hurriedly saying, "Give them two each and keep two in reserve for Fabian otherwise he'll end up throwing a tantrum, and that's the last thing that we need. If they ask you where you got them, tell them it's the... No! Put that down you two! It's perfectly fine where it is!"

Looking away from Viola and her two friends, Tristan instead carefully opened the tin to find three cellophane bags inside that held different flavoured biscuits. Carefully written on the front of each one was a name and a description of the flavour. Kelsey had chocolate and cream; Fabian had green tea cream; and Alban, though his name was written as Ali which made Tristan smile even more, had strawberry cream. The smell was wonderful and for a second Tristan was very tempted to try one but knew not to. These cookies were for the cubs and not for him.

Though he did make a note to ask Andrew to make him some, as they did look so tasty and he wanted to taste Andrew's cooking. It was rumoured to be delicious and the alpha wanted to try it for himself. Of course he would cook for the omega in return, as he had taken classes in the city and wanted to show off how independent he could be. No instant noodles for his family unless they all wanted it at the same time.

Taking a plate from the shelf, Tristan arranged the two sets of cookies as he had been instructed and added on the ones for Fabian should he happen to run into the cheeky scamp, though he was surprised that the triplets hadn't come running when they would have inevitably heard the tin opening. He supposed with so much going on in the garden, they were probably distracted. Placing the tin back in the cupboard, he found his smile growing wider. There were a couple of other cellophane packets with his and Daniel's name written on them hidden on the same shelf. Taking a deep breath and trying to control his feelings, Tristan headed back out into the garden.

Thankfully he wasn't waylaid too much this time as everyone was beginning to settle down into groups to talk and fill their stomachs with yet more food. Plus, from the smiles that he was receiving, many of the guests had figured out just what he was going to attempt to do so they were being kind and letting him go at his own pace. He wanted to make a good impression on the cubs, because he wanted them in his life just as much as he wanted Andrew too. Ideally they would all be together but that was a plan for the future. Baby steps needed to be taken first and that's what he planned to do.

Six

The Gingerbread Fairy

The playhouse at the bottom of the garden was a simple twelve-foot square building that was painted white, with red window frames and a little, red door. On the front of the door was a golden number 12 and a little knocker with a matching post box. Tristan's chocolate-black ears twitched as the alpha approached, clearly able to hear the two cubs engaged in some game and ducking down carefully, he glanced in through one of the windows to see what they were doing.

Alban was happily sitting on a brown bean bag chair with a large doll in his lap, who was wrapped up in a towel. He was delicately brushing the long strands of hair with a plastic comb with a contented expression on his face. Several sets of doll clothes were scattered around, along with a bottle and a tiny crib which rocked back and forth because Alban kept on knocking it with his elbow, though he did not appear to notice this. He was more focused on his doll, and it was an endearing sight to witness.

Kelsey meanwhile was playing with a large wooden train set, pushing it around the floor and making little choo-choo noises. They sounded adorable as he kept half singing a song which must have been from a kids show before going "Choo-choo!" really loudly and bringing the train to stop at the station, which was the toy box, where he would swap the passengers over.

The train was filled with bears, dolls, a couple of robots, dinosaurs, and a toy car but Kelsey talked to each toy as he put it into the box or into the train. As he was busy loading passengers, Kelsey wasn't paying attention to his surroundings, and so jumped in fright when Alban unexpectedly came up behind him and tapped him on the shoulder. Alban then presented his startled brother with the doll, which was now all dressed up in a bright pink outfit which made Kelsey's face light up with joy.

"Ali! You made her all pretty! Thank you!" Kelsey cried, hugging Alban before gently hugging his doll to his chest. "I'm going to make sure that Fabian never messes with you again. He's such a naughty boy, all cause he was mean to his doll and had it taken away. I'm going to put you up top then no one can get to you!"

Alban stood where he was, looking happy that Kelsey was smiling. It slightly shocked Tristan that Kelsey wasn't even looking at his brother when he was speaking but then figured that they were both littermates and could probably communicate better than anyone else in the family.

However, the small boy with soft, white hair and sable-black ears suddenly turned to look at him and blinked in surprise as finding an unfamiliar face at the window. Instead of panicking like Tristan expected him to, Alban just simply tilted his head one way and then the other before carefully raising his hands in front of himself. "Who are you?"

Tristan smiled and held up the plate of cookies. "I was sent by the gingerbread fairies to deliver these to Alban and Kelsey?"

That immediately made Kelsey appear beside his brother, who took one look at the offered cookies before quickly turning and making a sign towards Alban which the other nodded brightly at. Kelsey rushed forward to open the door and stepped out, looking at Tristan with interest before frowning. "You're not really from the fairies, are you?"

Raising an eyebrow in question, Tristan stared at the youngster. "Of course I am."

"Where's your wings then?" Kelsey said, sounding a little bratty but his eyes kept lingering on the cookies.

Tristan smiled, wanting to chuckle. "Ah, that would be telling. Wings don't always have to be visible for them to be there."

"That makes no sense," Kelsey said, standing his ground for the time being, though his eyes were firmly on the plate of treats. "All fairies have wings and... ow!"

Alban had stepped next to his brother and lightly pinched his ear in order to get him to stop talking before looking up at Tristan again with knowing eyes. "How did you get Vivi to give you those?" he asked, his hands moving a little slower as if he could sense that Tristan wasn't that good at sign language.

Or maybe he always automatically slowed it down whenever he met someone new, that was something that Tristan would certainly have to learn.

Kelsey, however, was kind enough to translate and Tristan laughed a little. "Aww, how did you rumble me so quickly?"

"Because Gingerbread Dragon always says that they're cookies from the Dragon Kingdom and not the land of fairies," Alban supplied again. This time the alpha was able to follow some of it himself. "Who are you?"

"I'm Tristan, your cousin who's just come back from the city," Tristan replied, smiling at the pair, and finger spelling his name. He had practiced sign language before returning but it was still not natural for him to use it. "It's nice to meet you two."

"Oh! You're the one who Vivi has been getting excited about," Kelsey said and then clambered forward, looking at him intently. "Though I don't see the spot."

"Spot?" Tristan asked, completely confused.

Kelsey nodded. "Vivi said that you have a spot on the end of your nose and it's not there."

For a few more seconds Tristan was completely confused as to what the youngster could be talking about and then he remembered. He shot a glare Viola's way as she added yet more food to the groaning table. Tristan wished that the whole spot incident could just be forgotten about, but apparently Viola was going to keep bringing it up for the rest of his life.

Right now, he wasn't going to think about it though, he had the cubs' attention and that was a good start. "Don't worry about the spot, Kelsey, it's Vivi's little joke and I'll get her back later for it. Now do you want these fairy... I mean... dragon cookies?"

"Yes please!" Kelsey said, bowing and holding his hand out for the plate whilst Alban made a sign of 'Thank you' before taking one of his cookies.

"Yah!" A loud voice rang out and suddenly Tristan found himself stumbling forward when Fabian lunged at him. "How come you get to give out dragon cookies to Kelsey and Ali but don't have any for me!"

Tristan was glad that the plate was safely in the hands of Kelsey otherwise the cookies would have fallen into the grass. Kelsey pouted at his brother. "Fabian is being a big meanie to Mister Tristan so he doesn't get his."

"Hey, no fair!" Fabian replied, looking annoyed. "You and Alban got yours!"

"Yes, because we're good boys and don't go pushing people around," Kelsey snapped back. "That means no dragon cookie for you."

"But I want my cookie!" Fabian started, looking to be on the verge of tears whilst Kelsey just looked furious, and Alban looked as though he couldn't figure out what was going on. Really, Tristan didn't know either, but he figured as strictly speaking he was the adult in charge he was going to have to be the one who was going to sort it out.

Thankfully he had dealt with Viola when she was being a million times more of a brat than Fabian was right now. From the videos that had been sent his way, he knew that the little omega who pretended to be an alpha most of the time had a perfect, exploitable soft spot. "Well, if you do want your cookie Fabian, then you're going to have to do something to earn it first."

"Earn it?" Fabian asked, looking bewildered. "But I always get dragon cookies... they're the best cookies in the whole, wide world."

"Oh, I don't doubt it," Tristan replied, still wanting desperately to try one of the cookies. He was sure that they would be delicious, and plus he was just a little envious of the fact that his boys had gotten to try their mother's cooking before he had had a chance. "But like Alban and Kelsey said, only good boys get dragon cookies and I've heard tales that you haven't been a good boy recently."

Fabian paled and blinked. "What do you mean, mister?"

Tristan smiled. "Well when I came to deliver the cookies, I heard that you had messed up Kelsey's doll because yours was taken away from you?"

A little gasp escaped from Fabian as he stepped back from Tristan, looking down in shame not a moment later. "I didn't mean to mess her up! I just wanted to play with her but she's so different from my doll that I got a little frustrated and I was going to put her back together again but Kelsey was coming and I didn't want him to be upset and mad with me cause I don't like it and..."

Kelsey stepped towards his brother. "Fabi, you could have just asked to borrow my doll. I would have shown you where everything was."

Fabian blinked and looked at his youngest brother. "But you were napping at the time, and I couldn't wake you."

"I wouldn't have minded being woken for that." Kelsey smiled, shaking his head.

Flattening his cupcake-white ears, Fabian still looked upset. "I know but still... I'm sorry Kelsey. I shouldn't have played with your doll and left her in that state."

A sudden squeak came from Fabian, who turned to find Alban standing just behind him with a concentrated look on his face as if he were pondering something. Fabian looked small and scared for a few seconds before his eyes lit up when Alban offered him a cookie from the plate. He then still lightly flicked the boy's forehead with his fingers. "Fabi can have one cookie for now cause me and Kelsey have had one. But he must play with us nicely for the rest of the afternoon to get the other cookie before bedtime. Is that okay, didi?" he asked, using a term of endearment meaning little brother.

Fabian nodded as he hugged the cookie to his chest and grinned cheekily. "Thank you Alban! Thank you, Tristan!" He chomped into the green tea cookie with relish and was clearly more than satisfied with its flavour. "But don't call me little! I'll be bigger than you one day, just you wait."

Chuckling a little at the trio, Tristan couldn't help but feel his heart melt a little as he watched the brothers interact. It was so easy to pick out the traits which they had gotten from Andrew, they were all so caring and loving but with a side that was quite unexpected. Tristan loved these cubs so much already and he had barely interacted with them.

"So, you three, since I've delivered your dragon cookies and you've all been good boys and eaten them, how about you tell me something about yourselves hmm?" Tristan asked, hoping his little ploy would work out for the best. "Because if I'm going to be around here often, I'm going to have to get to know you three pretty quick so we can play games together as friends!"

Fabian blinked. "Do we get to ask you questions in return?"

"Yes," Tristan said, smiling sweetly.

"About anything?" Kelsey asked next, his eyes wide. "And you'll respond truthfully to them all?"

Tristan nodded again, not considering where this conversation could go. "Yup, anything you want to know. Except anything too grown up, of course, because there are some things that only your... close family should tell you about." Tristan just caught himself before accidentally saying 'mother' or 'father' because he wasn't entirely sure if the cubs knew about the situation yet and it would be a little too heavy for a first time meeting.

Alban went first and asked, "Is your sign language good, Mister Tristan?"

"I'm learning, but I'm not too brilliant at it yet," Tristan replied honestly, once Fabian took his turn to translate but he smiled at the boy. "However your brothers have me covered so that should all be fine."

The triplets shared a knowing look between them before they all nodded to one another and then turned to look back at Tristan once again. Kelsey grinned. "Okay, you can start your twenty questions game with us Mister Tristan."

"Please call me Bobo. Mister sounds like I'm an old man," Tristan said, grinning back still completely unaware of what he was about to get dragged into. Bobo was a term that meant 'uncle', which was dancing around the truth - but he didn't know if they were ready to get into that yet.

"You are an old man," Fabian said cheekily, just ducking under a swipe that came from Kelsey and sticking his tongue out while making a bleh sound, but returned his attention to Tristan who was chuckling.

"I'm not that old, little one," Tristan said and ruffled Fabian's hair to annoy him. "But anyway. Let's begin. What are your full names and who's the eldest out of the three of you?"

Kelsey grinned brightly. "That's easy, Alban is the eldest, but he is nicknamed Ali by everyone. Then it's Fabian but we call him Fabi as well and then there's me, Kelsey. I'm the baby and I get called Kel but only by my gege's." Tristan recognised gege, another affectionate term meaning 'older brother'.

Alban let out a sound which could be counted as a laugh, before signing, "Everyone calls him Kuti though cause he's the cutest one out of us three."

Tristan smiled, "Ha, that makes sense."

"So, Bobo Tristan, how old are you?" Fabian asked, ignoring his brothers who were playfully squabbling over the 'Kuti' name.

Tristan smiled. "Well, I'm twenty-one in a few weeks' time."

"Wow, you really are old," Fabian said, and it took all of Tristan's mental strength to not chide the youngster in front of him. He had to remember that he was still young and innocent. "Though not as old as Aunt Paige and Uncle Paul, they're really really old."

Opening his mouth to argue, Tristan opted against it because really it was the truth. Just one that was better not being broadcast in front of his aunt and uncle. "Right, so for my next question, which school do you boys attend?"

"S.M. Academy Juniors," Fabian replied. "We're the top ranked students in our year."

"Not quite," Kelsey said. "There's a girl who beats us all the time in the rankings but she's super, super smart and it'd take someone with a bigger brain to beat her. Though we can beat her in club activities, we're the best there."

"Oh, what do you do for after school clubs?" Tristan asked, forgetting that really it should be the cubs turn to ask a question.

"Me and Fabi do dance classes and Alban goes to his wushu," Kelsey continued, grinning brightly, "It's the only time he'll wear his hearing aid though 'cause then he can hear the instructors if they're moving around or if he's in the middle of a fight."

Tristan blinked and turned to Alban. "You do martial arts?"

In reply Alban nodded. "Yes. I should be moving up to the intermediate class shortly."

That thought made Tristan's chest swell with pride. While he had never done any form of martial art outside of school, knowing that the eleven-year-old cub was already moving on to the intermediate class seemed like a very good sign.

Fabian grinned. "You should have been there months ago, but they wouldn't let you because of your age, Ali! Me and Kelsey are going in for a dance competition soon, Bobo Tristan. You'll have to come and cheer us on."

"Dance competition?" Tristan asked, blinking at the two boys.

"There's a reason they're called Dance Machines, Tristan," Paige called from a nearby table. "You'll have to go to practice with them one night after school. You'll be amazed by them."

Waving his thanks, Tristan smiled back at the trio. "Now that does sound fun! I look forward to seeing it."

Alban nodded and pondered for a few seconds about how to phrase his question before Kelsey translated it for him. "Alban wants to know what you do for a grown-up life."

Tristan smiled. "Well, until recently I was studying at university in the big city many miles from here. Now that I've finished, I've come home so that I can take up a job here in a local law firm and set about sorting out my adult life."

"In what way?" Alban asked, looking very curious once again.

A soft sigh escaped Tristan's lips. "Well I came back to help someone very special to me and I hope that I'll be able to take them as a mate and start a family together."

"Like Prince Charming?" Kelsey asked, his eyes all big, wide and innocent with his interpretation of adult life still being very much stuck in the fantastical realm of Shibi Movies. This was perfectly acceptable for an eleven-year-old by Tristan's standards.

He nodded in response. "Sort of. Just I don't have a big castle, or a huge bank account with lots of money and no access to fairy godmothers either, unfortunately."

"But you're going to work hard and make everything like that for your mate at some point, yes?" Fabian asked, his demeanour dropping a little which made him appear smaller and gentler. He looked adorable like this, so sweet and tender and clearly in need of some care for his little heart which made the cute nickname Fabi suddenly made sense.

Smiling contentedly, Tristan nodded his head. "Oh yes, I plan on doing that very much because I want my mate to be happy and able to do whatever he wants with his..."

Tristan's words were cut off as Alban suddenly appeared in front of his face, eyes even wider, more sparkling and innocent-looking than Kelsey's and Fabian's had appeared before. There was a look in them that sparked a mixture of wonder and worry in Tristan's heart. The look that Alban was giving him reminded him so much of the times when Andrew had looked at him as if he didn't quite believe that what he was seeing was real. Alban was saying something in sign language, but his hands were moving so fast that Tristan could barely keep up and neither could Kelsey from the confused expression on his face.

Fabian stepped up to pull Alban back a little bit, frowning at his brother with a sudden mature look about him. "Alban, don't go jumping to conclusions like that. We don't even know if the dragon is Mummy or not, we're only guessing." His words were spoken in a little whisper, obviously only meant for Alban to lipread but Tristan was close enough to hear his soft voice.

For a second Alban looked heartbroken but then he shook his head and pointed to Tristan again, making a sign which even though he had only just started the sign language classes, the elder was able to recognize.

It was the sign for 'Daddy'.

Seven

Will you be?

Whilst the party went on into the late hours of the night, Tristan could generally be found with three young cubs who appeared to be completely enthralled with him. A few of the party guests were a little bit unsure about someone of Tristan's age and status being able to engage so readily with them, but after a while it became apparent that there was no need to worry. Especially seeing as all three of the cubs started calling him Triba. Even when one of his distant uncles called him away to speak about his upcoming job or future prospects, the cubs let him out of their sight for maybe ten minutes before coming to drag him away.

It was insane to Tristan, that some alphas still viewed themselves as being the top of the hierarchy and able to dictate who could mate whom and dismiss any real chemistry. His distant uncle, a man called Guanyu who was viewed with disdain by everyone, seemed to be extra stuck up and wanted Tristan to mate with some rich omega of another family who would strengthen their territory. Guanyu was at the ripe, old age of forty-five, looking to retire early as he had more than enough money to do so. He had played the stock markets right when he was a lad and had made a fortune. There was unspoken disapproval about the fact that he had deliberately undercut several sale deals on companies, and then sold them on for an extortionate amount after stripping away all that was valuable. Tristan detested him because he was a creep who had always berated the young alpha even before his pre-presentation.

Guanyu was droning on and on about how he couldn't decide which of his illegitimate sons to leave the running of the company to, as his actual heir was a female who in his opinion was a waste of space. This was despite the fact that she ran the second most successful beauty retail brand in the country and invested nearly all of her profits into charities. Tristan didn't know what this all had to do with him but it seemed that it would be impossible to get away from Guanyu once he got his claws into a conversation.

However a small hand latched onto his finger and he turned to see a very sleepy looking, but teary-eyed Alban and instantly felt his heart break. "Aww, what's wrong Ali?" he asked gently, smiling politely towards the now-scowling Guanyu before scooping the young cub up into his lap and cuddling into him as if he were his own.

"Did you fall over or did Fabian push you into the wall again?" Tristan asked, making sure that Alban could see his lips but judging from his sleepy eyes, it was easy enough to guess what was wrong with the little youngster. "Ah, are you sleepy Ali? Is it time for you to be going to bed?"

"Huh, I don't know why they tolerate such a useless child around here," Guanyu said dismissively, glaring at Alban intently as if he were some kind of smear on the tip of his very expensive shoe. "The other two are charity cases, I suppose, but who would ever want to employ a deaf-mute I do not know. He'll be a drain on society by the time he's grown. In fact he's a drain on society now."

Glaring right back at the supposed alpha in front of him, Tristan wrapped his arms protectively around the tiny omega in his arms and fought back the urge to raise his hackles and growl. His inner alpha was furious that this old git would dare to insult his cub in front of him and was prepared to leap with the full intention to bite. Tristan kept himself outwardly calm and controlled though, as he had better weapons than claws. But his tea tree scent burnt with a fire that easily indicated just how pissed off he was towards the man speaking as if Alban wasn't sitting right there in his arms.

"At least Alban has a future that's far brighter than yours," he snorted towards the man. "I look forward to the day that all your evil, little schemes backfire on you so we can officially cast you out on the street and never have to deal with you ever again."

Standing up, Tristan shifted Alban more comfortably into his arms before sending one more poignant glare back towards his uncle. "If you ever dare to insult my cub again..."

Guanyu looked murderous. "That piece of filth is the product of a lowlife omega who allowed someone to take advantage of him. There is no family blood in him..."

"Go and stick your head up your own arse," Tristan shot straight back towards Guanyu. "He is mine! Just like Fabian and Kelsey are mine and no words of yours will ever change that fact."

"You're playing a dangerous game, boy," Guanyu snarled, slamming his glass down onto the table which drew all the more attention to their situation.

Thankfully Paul stepped up, placing a hand comfortingly onto Tristan's shoulder with a squeeze of warning. It was rare that Paul ever used his alpha presence, he was extremely meek and mild, many mistaking him for a beta. That was the thing with being a soft alpha. He wasn't naturally aggressive, and didn't dominate because he never needed to.

However, insulting his family was a way to make sure that he unleashed hell.

"Tristan, take Alban to bed will you?" Paul spoke with a soft tone, "I need to have to a word with my brother-in-law that I don't want a cub to hear."

Nodding, Tristan sent a final glare towards Guanyu, along with an harsh wave that was under no illusion of being anything but rude as it showed off the mating mark on his hand clear as day, before heading back towards the house. He felt Alban move ever so subtly, resting against him with a nuzzle that was both adorable and grounding. Without meaning to, Tristan scented the cub back, having to smile when his tea tree mixed with the baby milk smell in such a perfect way. A slight whiff of caramel appeared for a few seconds but it was gone the next instant.

Tristan smiled and scented his cub harder, longing to keep that beautiful scent hidden for just a while longer. He knew eventually it would come out, as it had to do but it made his inner alpha so full of pride that the cub had chosen him to share this precious little secret with. So proud in fact that he walked into the back door leading to the house, bashing his head off the side of it.

"Ow," Tristan complained, before hearing rushing feet coming towards him.

Kelsey reached just up above his waist but was hopping up and down on his feet, whilst making grabby hands towards the alpha. "Want Triba!

Daniel chuckled from the bottom of the stairs. "There, you got your Triba, now come on up to bed."

"Uppie!" Kelsey pouted in a way that was way too adorable for an eleven-year-old but made Tristan smile all the same.

"Kelsey," Daniel said with a voice filled with the patience of a man who had had to deal with the cubs for a touch too long. He chuckled when Tristan slightly repositioned Alban and then picked up Kelsey as if he weighed nothing. The alpha looked way too proud of himself for being able to hold both cubs like this and the platinum-haired elder just rolled his eyes in fond exasperation.

Alban was already practically asleep, chewing absently on Tristan's collar, whereas Kelsey simply snuggled up to the alpha and tried to pretend that he wasn't falling asleep.

"Where's Fabian?" Tristan asked, glancing around and wondering just how he was going to carry three youngsters all in one go even though he was more than convinced that he could manage it.

Daniel smiled. "Little tear away is already in bed. Come on, they sleep up here."

Nodding Tristan followed Daniel up the stairs and after a moment had to let out a spontaneous chuckle as reality struck. He had just claimed the cubs in front of his distantly related uncle who was known to be a terrible, old-fashioned alpha who involved himself in things which were never good. "Don't know where that bravery came from."

Daniel just chuckled. "Old git deserved it and Paul's been looking for an excuse to kick him out of family gatherings for years. Plus he did insult your cub so it's perfectly fine to put the git back in his place."

Tristan replied with a tight smile. "Though I think Aunty will be having words with me later."

"Ha, she'll more than likely be congratulating you on putting that old geezer where he should be," Daniel said, pausing so that he could run his fingers through Alban's thick, white hair, "Fancy saying our little Ali is worthless? I'm sure he could probably run the company better than any of that man's offspring, excluding Jessica of course."

Tristan nodded, his ears fluffing up with pride. "That I don't doubt. I'm not worried about my Alban, I'm sure that he'll be able to do whatever he wants to do in the future, and he'll be one of the best at it."

For a few seconds Daniel was silent, his slate-grey ears flattening for a moment whilst his tail twitched. Then he brightened up, his fur taking on a sheen almost immediately. "Well, if I didn't already know that you were Andrew's mate, I would have definitely just confirmed it now."

A frown rippled across the other alpha's face. "What do you mean by that?"

"You just said 'My Alban'." Daniel chuckled. "It means you see them as your own already."

Rolling his eyes skyward, Tristan couldn't help but let out a disgruntled sound at his friend. "Well of course. What do you take me for? Some idiot who would only accept the mother but not the cubs? I went out in that rain storm to find them and I kept them safe, you should have known then that I would never even dream of saying they weren't mine."

If Tristan hadn't already been carrying the cubs, Daniel would have given the other alpha a push for his remark, as talking about that night was something no one really liked to do too much. "Oh hush, just you wait until they start finding potential mates and see how your hormones react then, Daddy."

"Shush," Tristan hissed quietly towards Daniel though he was trying not to burst out into joyful laughter right now. "You'll wake them up."

"Trust me, they wouldn't wake up even if we were in the middle of a thunderstorm," Daniel said, shifting to take Alban so that Tristan was only left with Kelsey in his arms. "Now you can deal with putting Kelsey to bed while I sort Alban out. He gets a bit fussy when he's sleepy and it's best we train you with the easiest one."

A little snore stopped Tristan from asking about Fabian, as he turned to see the cub sleeping heavily in his bed. He wore yellow pyjamas and was so deep into dreaming that his little, white ears kept twitching every now and again. It was undeniably adorable and it was so tempting to just snap a picture but the alpha's hands were rather full at the moment. Instead he surveyed the rest of the room, noting that whilst it was small, it perfectly accommodated the three cubs.

Three of the four walls had been turned into separate areas with a bed pushed up against each one, which had its own little table at the end which held a nightlight. To the right of each bed were a set of drawers and each area clearly reflected the personality of each little cub.

Fabian slept under a pink, cotton cover with white flowers on, whilst clutching to a dragon plushie. On the wall by his bed were a lot of posters. Some idols, others action series, others homely series, one 'High Paw Musical' poster and a bunch of photographs of family and friends. His bed was covered in plushies and there were action figures of robots and some fashion wolf dolls on top of his dresser as well.

Alban had shelves filled with books, comics and manga in a mismatched set up that just seemed to be perfectly fitting. There was also a shelf of tiny little houses that looked to be handmade as they lit up with gentle lights that offered a sweet glow. On top of his dresser were yet more books, along with several trophies and medals that appeared to be related to martial arts and a pair of football boots were on the floor next to the bed. His bedsheets were a dark purple with glow-in-the-dark stars on them and he had a nightlight as well.

Kelsey was a more eclectic mix with several plant pots that were blooming with fresh flowers, a bunch of art supplies on top of the drawers and at least five sketch books stacked in an unorganised fashion. His walls had posters of idols, dancers and a smaller, more neatly organised, bookshelf that seemed to be intently focused on studies more than anything. The bedding was of Bob the Fish Captain from 'Space Buddiez' and there was an imitation fish bowl that acted like a night light too.

Turning to look back at Kelsey, Tristan smiled gently and tapped the boy on his nose. "Now, little one, let's get you ready for bed, hmm?"

The cub yawned and sat down on the bed, starting his routine of getting undressed whilst Tristan went to find pyjamas. Thankfully Daniel took pity on him and indicated where it would be silently, as he helped Alban get sorted out as well. Soon a tired Kelsey was dressed in a Canine Pup onesie, looking even more adorable than before. Tristan couldn't resist grabbing the floppy ears and pulling them over the pup's rose-white ears to then playfully cover his eyes. "Peek-a-boo."

The cub laughed and batted at the elder's hand, before letting out a yawn and leaning forward so he could rest up against the alpha with a sigh. Tristan allowed himself a moment to just embrace the pup, petting his head gently. "There, you ready to go to sleep now, Kelsey?"

Nodding his head, Kelsey allowed himself to be picked up whilst Tristan gently pulled back the covers and set the boy down on the pillows. "Goodnight Kelsey," the alpha said softly, running his hand gently down the side of the cub's head as his eyelids drooped closed.

"Night... Daddy..." Kelsey replied quietly, the last word really too faint for any of them to hear but both alphas knew what had been said.

Feeling his heart swell, Tristan moved across to Fabian to check that the youngster was safely in the land of dreams before pressing a kiss to his temple. "Nanight Fabi, pleasant dreams." A light hum was his response and Tristan smiled before carefully moving away.

Alban was sitting up in bed, unlike the other two he wore a long-sleeved nightdress in a light blush-pink with white lace on the collar and cuffs. Tristan thought he looked absolutely adorable. The thought occurred of what Andrew slept in, would he be in pyjamas or a long flowing nightgown? Pushing those thoughts away as quickly as they appeared, Tristan refocused on the eldest of the cubs with a smile.

Alban held his arms out for a hug and Tristan embraced him happily before pulling back.

"Thank you," Alban signed to him, smiling brightly though it was clear that he was about to pass out from exhaustion.

"For what?" Tristan asked slowly in reply, glad he had picked up a few signs.

Daniel thankfully translated the next bit. "For telling the mean uncle to stay away."

For a second Tristan was confused and then realized that with the way that Alban would have been in his arms he would have been able to easily read his lips. A blush crossed his cheeks but he smiled, reaching out to run his hand over the boy's soft, black ears. "I would do it in a heartbeat Alban, no one has the right to say anything like that to you or the others."

For a second Alban hesitated but then took a deep breath. "Did you mean it when you said I was your cub?"

This time Tristan was prepared and he nodded slowly. "Yes. I meant every word. You and your brothers."

A smile broke across Alban's lips, his ears perking right up. "Will you promise to make Mama really happy and come play with us?"

"How do you..." Tristan started before realising that probably Andrew's cubs knew more about Andrew than he about them. Which was heartbreaking but understandable. Still the alpha had to smile. "I promise Alban. It may take a lot of time and you'll have to be patient, but I want us all to be one big, happy family."

A sort of high-pitched squeal came out of the cub who launched himself forward, wrapping a tight hug around Tristan's neck and squeezing tightly. Even though he didn't express it with words or signs,

Tristan knew that the cub was thanking him profusely right now and that made him feel like he was on top of the world. After a minute or two, he pushed Alban back and gently rubbed his nose against the cub's. "Now it's sleepy time, Ali," Tristan said softly, laying the youngster down onto his pillows, "You've got to join your brothers in dreamland."

Alban nodded his response and smiled, before signing, "Goodnight, Daddy."

"Goodnight Alban," Tristan said softly, leaning down to press a kiss to his forehead and made sure that Alban was all wrapped up in his blankets before rising and quietly heading out of the bedroom with Daniel.

He saw the question coming a mile off and waited until the door had clicked shut before letting out a little sigh. "I think your nephews have been putting the pieces together a lot quicker than Andrew would ever suspect."

A confirming hum came from Daniel. "It would appear so. However, I don't know if you'll ever be able to give Alban what he wants from family life. Meetups are one thing, living together as one family is another all together."

"I know, but we've got plenty of time, and no rush," Tristan said softly in reply. Thoughtfully he tilted his head to the side. "He's got his hospital appointment tomorrow, right?"

"Yeah, for the blockers treatment," Daniel said with a sigh. "They may take him off them soon."

Tristan nodded, "Good, it's about time he started having a regular cycle. It'll help him out a lot, I'm sure of it."

"You're not thinking of going with him to that, are you?" Daniel asked, eyeing the other alpha up warily. Mate or not, there were some things which still had to be kept private.

Tristan shook his head. "Hell no. I'm not just going to barge into his private affairs like that. You make me sound like a sex deprived pervert."

"Well, it was just..." Daniel started but was interrupted by Tristan.

"I told him I would take him to the cat-sith café that he loves for breakfast tomorrow, after the appointment," Tristan said, rolling his eyes slightly before smiling. "Keep it simple and give us some time alone in a setting that's typical for a first date."

About to argue the fact that the other had clearly been watching too many dramas or reading too many soppy romance stories, Daniel instead shut his mouth when he realised that for an first actual date something as simple as going to a cafe would be ideal for Andrew. Especially the cat-sith café that he already adored. It wouldn't be too much pressure and it would be cute with easy exit options should the omega's anxiety get too high.

A groan left Daniel as he started down the stairs. "Stop being so perfect for my little brother, I can't kick your ass if you're this good!"

Laughing aloud, Tristan grinned and chased Daniel down the stairs, he needed to let off some steam and Daniel was the perfect alpha who could help him out with that. Plus they had to track down Paul and get the low-down on what had happened with Guanyu, and then maybe finish off the beer and roll about on the floor like idiots for an hour or two.

Eight

The Secrets We Keep

The scratch of pencil on paper had always been a soothing sound to Andrew. Though he was very aware that his drawings were not masterpieces, they were just for a bit of fun. It was something that one of the child psychologists had gotten him to do, a sort of release for his pent up emotions. While sometimes no one could really get the point of what it was that the young cub was trying to express, they praised his artwork and encouraged him to keep doing it. These days Andrew drew when he was waiting to visit Doctor Smith, as it was something to pass the time when he couldn't be bothered with his phone and it kept him from focusing on his anxiety about entering the room beyond.

He knew very well that there was nothing in there that was going to hurt him. He understood that the tests were to make sure that he was healthy enough so that they could take him off the blockers to allow him to fall into a more natural omega cycle. But knowing that still didn't make it any easier.

The very idea that he could go back into heat, a time where he was completely vulnerable and unable to process anything, was utterly terrifying to Andrew. Usually the mere thought would trigger memories of what had happened all those years ago, even if he did try to suppress them. It had been noted to be very unhealthy to completely lock away such trauma but every time they had tried to make him face it, things had not gone well. Andrew hated the idea of being in heat ever since his first time and never wanted to go through it again if he could avoid it.

However, the omega also knew that if he wanted to mate fully with Tristan, then he'd have to go into heat as it was the safest way to do so. A mating bite was painful to deliver, so both parties being in the adrenaline-fueled rush of excitement of a heat made things a lot easier and gave the alpha a chance to properly show how they could care for their omega. Andrew knew that his alpha would only ever treat him with respect, love and the most gentle of touches. He had proved that throughout the years, even when they had both been far too young to really understand what had happened on that night in the rain. The mating mark that Tristan bore was only half of the promise that had been made that night, they weren't fully mated yet but Andrew didn't know if he could realistically take the bite.

It was a big, scary thought to the champagne-white wolf and something that he had extensively talked to his therapist about in the lead up to Tristan's return.

Which surprisingly, felt right to the omega.

He had initially been very worried that he would just be a nuisance, that Tristan would be bringing someone else home on his arm and he'd be left abandoned like he should have been all those years ago. But the alpha had just stayed where he was meant to be, smiling so warmly at him as if his mere presence filled a gaping void in his heart. Andrew did not want to believe in silly stories, those romances that he occasionally indulged in when he thought no one was really paying any attention.

But the plain truth was, that even as overemphasised as they were, it was all very true.

The omega smiled to himself, unaware of just how love-struck and smitten he looked but honestly he wouldn't have minded if anyone had mentioned it. He felt good thinking about Tristan, about realising that the alpha was trustworthy and honest, that maybe one day they would be mates. It was all still very new in an oddly familiar way. The young wolf was almost unable to comprehend all the grown-up emotions when it just felt like he was back in the days of long summer afternoons. When the little alpha would play with him in the back garden and good-naturedly fend off his protective elder brother. Maybe it was just as things were meant to be, that they were still the cubs that had met in the storm, and fate had entwined them all together at that point.

For a moment he paused in his drawing, wondering just what it all meant. Immediately he took in a long, deep breath, forcing down the panic attack that wanted to burst out of his chest and instead looked down at his drawing. To his slight bemusement, he found that he had drawn a very wonky castle with turrets and flags, surrounded by a moat. The surrounding fields were just large pencil marks with shaded bits to represent paths. There was a rather blobby-looking dragon laying near the bottom of the castle, close to the drawbridge and just opposite it was another blobby-looking dragon but with the addition of three smaller blobs that had yet to show any real signs of having a design applied to them.

Andrew paused as he stared at them, feeling the familiar anxiety start to clench at his heart when he thought about his cubs. It was a clawing intensity that made the omega want to immediately rub away the smaller blobs because he was terrified that he would never be good enough to represent them. He had never been there for them, never taken care of them like he should have. He was a failure as a mother and an omega and he should never give them a second thought. But Andrew did. He cared so much for those three little bundles even if he could only watch them from afar. Of course the omega understood that he had been a child when they came into his life. There was nothing he could have done to provide for them as everything he needed only came later when his body matured. As a wolf he had matured far too quickly due to an incorrectly treated infection, which had stunted his developing instincts.

That didn't mean he didn't care about his cubs. He wanted them to have good, happy lives and was more than thankful that Paige and Paul had taken them in to raise them. They were good parents to the cubs, making sure that everything was just as it was meant to be. Andrew couldn't be happier to know that they were safe, and when his curiosity got to him, the two wolves had been more than happy to allow him whatever access he wanted without becoming too pushy over the subject. Daniel kept an eye on them too, wanting to ensure that his nephews got the best start in life and always offered Andrew updates and photos whenever he could.

Andrew did not know if there would ever be a day when he would actually meet the cubs in person, but for now he was content to be the distant 'Gingerbread Dragon'.

Shaking his head to dispel all these thoughts, Andrew made a clicking sound with his tongue. "Leave it for another day." Closing the drawing pad, he left the indistinct dragon blobs and went to grab his bag from underneath his seat. Only for the strap to catch on a chair leg and spill half the contents on the floor. Andrew blushed bright red at the mess, then let out a sigh and started picking up the items that were scattered about, glad that he was the only person in the room. There was his phone; a pencil case; the headphones he had brought to listen to music to but forgot to charge; several receipts; his LunaTrix 'Space

Buddiez' purse; a selection of fidget toys that the wolf got to keep himself occupied if he did not have a drawing pad to hand; three capsule pods; and the keychain photocard holder that held an image of Tristan and Andrew when they were fourteen and had gone to the 'Space Buddiez' theme park.

It had been a little overwhelming that day, as Andrew had not been the best with crowds but Tristan had stuck by his side, gone on all the slow rides with him and even bought him ice cream to make sure that he was happy and having fun. The only big ride they had gone on was a rollercoaster which Andrew had surprisingly enjoyed so much that he had asked to go on a second and a third time. Of course his alpha had indulged him even if he ended up being sick afterwards. They also had a photograph from a very sweet attraction, where it was possible to get photos taken at iconic spots from the show and Andrew had chosen the picnic scene. It was a very cute spot and the photo was even cuter so Andrew had gotten to keep it.

Andrew always carried it with him, though he kept it secret from everyone else.

Settling back down in his chair with a sigh, Andrew suddenly frowned and grabbed his bag to pull out the three capsule pods. He did not usually keep capsule pods in his bag, as he liked to open them in the stores and return the pods as quickly as possible. The omega's ears flicked in confusion as he ran his hands over the designs, an unusual black colour with golden symbols all over them, realising that they were all from the 'Red Force' series which was based off a cartoon about twelve young wolves who inherited powers from an ancient tree of life to become dragon-wolf hybrids.

It just happened to be Andrew's absolute favourite show and he had been desperate to collect all twelve members, as he only had two of them, being the Shenlong and Qilin. But even finding the capsule machines with them was next to impossible. They were also unusually expensive, even for one capsule. So to have three suddenly appearing in his bag was not something that the young omega knew how to deal with.

Except a minute later when he started to open the pods.

Inside he found the Azure Dragon, the Turtle Dragon and the Rainbow Dragon.

The three youngest members from the original cartoon lineup who were all considered to be highly cherished and rare. Andrew held the figures, marvelling at the craftsmanship that had gone into them and the sheer beauty. Tears stung at his eyes, because he honestly never thought that he would get to hold them in his hands. Though his heart ached as he picked up the gentle scent of baby milk that was just tinged with syrup bubbles, caramel and bubble gum.

Pausing for a moment, the omega hugged the figures to his chest before grabbing his phone to text to his elder brother.

To Daniel:

Did you tell my cubs about Red Force?

To Andrew:

What?

Oh, you found them.

-grin-

To Daniel:

Did you tell them?

To Andrew:

Nope. Not me.

To Daniel:

Then how did they know about the capsules? The show isn't even on anymore.

To Andrew:

Gingerbread Dragon sent them each a stationery pack of the main Red Force characters last year for their birthday.

"Andrew, it's your appointment time," came the familiar and welcoming voice of Megan, the receptionist who had been at the therapist's office for as long as Andrew could recall.

The omega started and looked up, blushing a little before gathering his things into his bag and heading into the familiar room, his mind absolutely boggling with this new information. Had he really done such a thing? Sharing an old TV series with his cubs when they probably had never even heard of it. When did he even get hold of three stationery sets from that old series dew how did he not have one of his own? He would have treasured something like that without question, but he shared it willingly with his cubs. So much so that they had somehow tracked down three of the hardest capsule figures to find and somehow sneaked them to him.

Daniel was involved, there was no other explanation, as Andrew didn't go near his cubs. But the omega wasn't angry at his brother.

"Something on your mind?" asked Doctor Smith, already pouring the tea into the green, ceramic cups that Andrew liked using as they made a lovely little clink sound when placed back on the saucer. It was a legend that the clink of a cup and saucer would make the wolf goddess Amarok very happy and willing to listen to all your concerns for an hour or two without complaint. It was something that all therapists used, as they said it invited the goddess's spirit in to soothe the patients. Andrew always felt less on edge when he heard that sound and would sometimes allow his gaze to drift towards the window where an old chair would be left with a small coffee table that always had a cup, a vase of flowers and a plate of small sweets on it.

Wolves didn't have churches or monuments to their goddess, she lived in the houses, towns and cities right by everyone's side, able to be called upon at a moment's notice or to intervene when required.

Andrew thought about his response for a few long seconds and then quietly responded with, "I... I think the... my cubs... know about me?"

Doctor Smith, an older beta with greying fur, observed him silently for a moment with a gentle look through his round glasses. He hummed at length and took a long sip of the tea, a light green tea mix today. "What does that make you feel?"

"Terrified," Andrew answered immediately, "but in a way that makes me hopeful?"

The beta watched Andrew duck his head down with a blush. Doctor Smith had worked with Andrew for many years and was always glad to see the progress that the omega made in regards to his natural instincts. They had always been there, even if the young wolf had tried to deny them, and now that he was beginning to be in a stage of life where he could act upon them it was a lovely outcome. He just had to be careful about the words he chose to use in the next few minutes. Silence was probably the best option, as in a moment Andrew would try to fill it so that he could voice his opinions without having to be asked for it directly.

"I mean," started Andrew not five seconds later, "I guess that they'll have been aware of me, that I'm still alive and just... unable to visit them. But I never thought that they'd... that my cubs would want... to meet me."

"Cubs naturally gravitate to their birth givers," Doctor Smith replied in his smooth, professional style. "Part of it's natural instinct, another is the call of the pack bond and..."

"But I abandoned them!" Andrew managed to say with a touch of anger, his voice raised a little higher than normal, but not enough to alert anyone outside. The omega was generally quiet and soft spoken, always afraid to rock the boat. Doctor Smith made a note of this but allowed Andrew the time to continue ranting. "I left them when they needed me the most and I barely interact with them except for letters and cookies and..."

Again his head dropped down low. "I can't be their mother, as much as they may want me to be."

For a moment or two, Doctor Smith was quiet before he asked, "What if they just wanted to meet you, to create a relationship with you. Have you ever considered something like that?"

This time Andrew thought long and hard about the question because when framed as it now was, it made sense in his head. His cubs had a mother, they had Paige who had looked after them their entire lives. They had a big sister in Viola who bossed them around, ensured they got to school on time and generally kept up with their chores and housework. They had a father in Paul, as well as aunts, uncles and cousins and a whole family to call their own. Maybe they did just want to meet him, to bring him into their lives not because they had some basic instinct to bond with their birth mother, but because they wanted him there. To be a member of the family, a member of the pack. It was an option that he had never considered, even on the day when he had come up with Gingerbread Dragon and started sending the three of them letters and cookies.

The omega's tail started wagging just the tiniest bit at the thought that maybe he did not have to fully be a mother to the cubs. Maybe he just needed to be there for them, to take part in their lives in the capacity that he could manage. Maybe that's what the cubs wanted as well. Not him to replace the family that they already had, but to be a piece of it.

"What if it's just me jumping to conclusions?" he asked, in a more level and polite tone than his last outburst.

Doctor Smith shook his head, "No, Andrew. You're not jumping to conclusions. You're working off presumptions that are influenced by your own past, which is a symptom of what you went through. Most cubs are curious from a young age, always wanting to seek answers to questions on a multitude of topics. And to be honest, I wouldn't be surprised if your boys are not already asking questions to the adults who know about their mother. They've probably been asking them longer than you have been accepting pictures and videos of them, but those who know will have kept it from you so that you weren't hurt by it."

Instinctively Andrew pulled out his phone and scrolled to a shared file which was updated daily by most of the pack members. There were tons of photos of Alban, Kelsey and Fabian, doing all sorts of things, as well as videos, voice clips, little stories and copies of certificates or awards that were all being stored in one place so that when they were old enough, they could have the password and a whole history of their lives before them. Andrew had initially been reluctant to connect to it, the invite had remained unopened in his inbox for the better part of a year before finally he had joined in and cried a river of tears. His cubs were beautiful, silly and growing up so well.

He had photos of their birthdays, of award nights, silly little moments that were too precious not to share. Best of all, there was a file dedicated to Gingerbread Dragon which had started off small but was steadily growing. Each excited reaction, each art project completed and each cookie rated for taste and time lasted (which was never long once the cubs knew they had arrived), was all there for him to see and enjoy whenever he wanted. Could it be that the cubs knew he had access? Or that they'd want him to have access?

But how would he ever be able to explain that he had them at eight years old? The omega's gingerbread scent took on a smoky hint of burning in his disappointment, at realising the inevitable truth. He could never tell them how they came to be, because it was too traumatising,

"How can they even begin to understand, though?" Andrew spoke out loud, his shoulders and ears drooping completely. "What I went through to have them, what I should have never gone through... I can't even... I hate..."

"I did not mean that they would be asking about what happened to you," Doctor Smith replied softly, causing Andrew to look up at him with a question in his eyes. "Like all cubs, they want to see their parents when times are harsh or they don't understand the world because it is very hard to replace that feeling of love and contentment which comes between the bond between mother and cub. Whilst Paige has done an amazing job in raising the cubs as her own, they're at the age now where they begin to realize how different the bond is between the different pack members and they'll want to know where their missing piece is."

"Pieces," Andrew corrected automatically before choking on his own self-inflicted acid-reflux. Doctor Smith was quick to give him tissues, along with a glass of water and had more than enough patience to allow the omega to settle down. He allowed his warming tea scent to fill the room, to offer comfort to the shivering form opposite him. The doctor had to take a moment to remind himself he needed to act professionally. Part of his primal instincts were furious at the pathetic excuse for an alpha who had committed such a hideous crime against his patient. Anyone else would have done the sensible thing and gotten the cub to a hospital instantly instead of letting him suffer that night, and for many nights since. He was angry on Andrew's behalf, but for the sake of his recovery, Doctor Smith couldn't let it show.

Thankfully the omega calmed down quickly, taking many sips of his tea and began playing with a pet rock which he had gotten from a wild excursion when he was twelve. It had a couple of googly eyes on it, was a deep grey colour but contained some kind of natural crystal which years upon years of handling had revealed. It was only palm-sized and perfect for times like these when Andrew needed to connect naturally back to the wilds. Doctor Smith noted that his alpha mate should be informed to take him for a run in their wild forms as it would deepen the bond between the pair.

"I think you only have to worry about the singular of your previous statement, Andrew," Doctor Smith continued once he was certain that the omega opposite him was in a good place to continue their conversation.

"How can you say that?" Andrew asked, feeling a shuddering palpitation through his heart as his mind drifted very briefly over to thoughts about that man and the terrible things that he had done.

"In all of our sessions, I have never heard any stories of the cubs taking an interest in anyone but you," Doctor Smith replied, pulling up a couple of records on the computer as a way of allowing some time for Andrew to think over his words. "Usually this means that there is no bond created, and given the circumstances of how you were found, it is easy to conclude that they have no care for anyone but their mother."

A long silence passed as Andrew processed this information, allowing himself to go through the emotions as they came to him while he gently rubbed at the smooth surface of his pet rock. Doctor Smith fell into a recognisable silence, checking through the reports and findings from the omega's last medical check up to see how the reduction of the suppressants was affecting him. Everything was looking good, no major side effects noted as of yet which was great to see. Staying on suppressants was generally a bad thing. Even those who wanted to be betas for a while had to be monitored after a certain point but medically it could be managed very well. Andrew was doing everything that he had been requested to and the results were almost textbook which was a big relief to the doctor who still triple checked anything before moving on to the next phase.

Andrew started flipping back through the pictures of the cubs on his phone, finding a smile crossing his face. One of Alban painting a picture but getting most of the paint all over himself; another of Kelsey and Fabian at their latest dance recitals; and one of games in the play house. There was also one of everyone in funny costumes at an All Hallows' Eve party, before the hilarious shots of the family running through an haunted house attraction and getting scared witless by pretend zombies and ghosts. Andrew would never survive a haunted house. He would be a jabbering wreck before he even got through the door.

A sudden, desperate curiosity grabbed him and once again he messaged his elder brother, who always seemed to be a font of knowledge when it came to the cubs

To: Daniel

Have the cubs ever asked about their father?

To: Andrew

What? Why are you asking about that?

To: Daniel

Please, I just want to know.

To: Andy

No. Never. Even when they were tiny. They asked for you but now I think about it... never that thing.

To: Daniel

Only about me?

To: Andy

Yes! They love the whole Gingerbread Dragon creation you came up with and they want to come visit you or have you visit them because they're so curious about you.

Wait, didi, are you wanting them to meet you or both you and Tristan?

To: Daniel

Thanks.

Sitting back in his chair, Andrew let out a breath and felt the urge to start crying all over again but he couldn't honestly say why. Was he happy over the fact that his cubs had no interest in their biological father or something else? His mind was a blaze with a million different questions, all of which he was sure to find a very obvious answer to if he were to simply ask. At the same time there was that ever-present worry that built up in his stomach.

Though not even a few seconds later, his phone blipped again and he picked it up to find another message from Daniel.

To: Andy

You know... I didn't say anything the other day but Fabian asked me if your birthday was November 5th or 6th because he wanted to send you something. I asked him how he knew and he just gave that usual cheeky smile of his so I never got the answer out of him.

It was followed by another blip a few seconds later.

To Andy:

It's odd, ever since those three little terrors found out about Tristan coming home they've been going on non-stop about you. I didn't even notice the change in their behaviour now that I come to think about it. Hopefully it's nothing but... now I'm getting worried about it.

Andrew chuckled and smiled, before typing back a quick reply to his elder brother.

To: Daniel
Don't worry about it.
I guess I should have seen this coming.
To: Andrew
Do you want me to arrange a meet for you and your cubs?

Locking the phone again, Andrew ignored the last message entirely and instead let out a long sigh towards the doctor who was looking at him with a silent question. "I guess my cubs are better at finding out about me than I am about them."

"The inquisitive minds of youth are always the most adaptable," Doctor Smith said with a smile. "What do you feel about that?"

Andrew heaved in a breath, paused and then released it before shaking his head. "I don't know. I really don't."

"It never crossed your mind?" Doctor Smith pressed softly. "How they might want to see you?"

"A couple of times," Andrew admitted softly. "But they're still so young and with so many adventures ahead of them. I thought that I would just be... something forgotten in the back of their minds. A little shoe box that they would find one day and explore later because..."

Doctor Smith gently filled the silence that followed the cut off sentence. "You were never deemed to be a bad mother, I do hope you know that."

"What?" Andrew asked surprised, his ears raising up to a high point before flattening fully down like a child who had been scolded. "I can't be anything but."

"By all standards, for your age when things occurred, you actually did the best job you could," Doctor Smith started soothingly.

Andrew shook his head as he interrupted, "But I am a bad mother. I can't even bring myself to hold them, to talk to them. The very idea that they've found out anything about me is terrifying and just makes me want to run away to the city or... my babies don't need me to mess up everything. They don't need to have me as a burden on their lives... I want them to grow up good and pure and be everything that I couldn't be. How can I do that if I end up in their lives?"

Doctor Smith let out a soft sigh. "Andrew, I'm going to tell you something that is completely off the record. Knowing you as well as I do, I know that you will not believe me for a long time but one day my words will come back to you, and you will realize why I am saying them today. I have met many different mothers and fathers over the years, some who are apparently perfect in every way and who just want the best for their cubs, like you do, but without the skills or the self realisation that the problem with their cub is themselves. Because they put too much pressure on their cub, think that they should act in a certain way even though they never brought them up correctly to begin with and live in a world of fantasy. You, however, are one of the strongest omegas that I have ever met. You were put in a situation that you should have never been exposed to, forced into something that you were not mentally or even physically ready for and yet never once have you blamed your cubs for that, or their existence or wished that they were dead. Your only wish for them was that they would grow up healthy, happy and surrounded by love and affection."

He paused for a fraction of a second to take a sip of his tea. "Yes, you have not been with them, have not seen their first steps or physically taken care of them in the middle of the night when they're awake with a screaming fever, but you have always loved them. Whilst it has taken you time to accept that fact and to gain your confidence in wanting to see them, you have always been hovering in the background, watching and waiting just to make sure that nothing bad ever happens to them. I'm not going to claim that you're the world's most perfect mother, but in your own right, you are a very strong mother who works through every day to reach his end goal."

Andrew blinked in surprise towards the man. "You honestly believe I can do that?"

Doctor Smith's nod was serious and confident. "I'm not expecting you to suddenly turn up at their doorstep tomorrow morning to give them hugs and kisses but within the next two years, I can see you seeing them at least once a week for a family meet up or something similar."

"How do you know that?" Andrew asked, his voice barely a whisper once again.

There came a knowing smile from Doctor Smith. "Because you are already interacting with them, you're too curious about them and want the best of the best for them. You want your future mate to accept them as his own, just as much as you are his and he is yours. That is the sign of someone who is more than prepared to accept cubs into their lives, you just have to have the confidence to take that first step. Which will be the biggest step forward for you, but one that is achievable now."

This block of information hit Andrew like a tidal wave, but it felt like it was controlled and gentle. More like the wave machines at the water park, rather than the brutality of the waves out at sea. Andrew had never convinced himself that he could ever be this close to any of this, but it was a truth that was now presented to him, and made perfect sense. It was still frightening, but it was true nonetheless.

"Hmm, it seems that you're having no adverse side effects from reducing the suppressants. I think we should be able to reduce the dose further to just one tablet a day and hopefully start your natural cycle functioning in a proactive manner... though your dopamine levels are still a little low but I'm hoping that will improve with your alpha's help." Doctor Smith said, noting that their time was beginning to run short and he did need to get the next stage of the omega's medical underway.

"You mean... I'll be getting heats?" Andrew asked, completely missing the latter part of the doctor's explanation.

"Not quite, the lower suppressant should still work on those," Doctor Smith said, "but you may become a little more receptive to your partner at times. Perfectly natural of course and as a doctor, I would recommend keeping things within the more gentle side of sexual activities. Penetration would not be recommended but oral and touches should be more than enough stimulation for now."

Andrew had gone bright red at those words and hid his face with his hands, but Doctor Smith continued. "Though from what I've heard of your potential mate, I think you should just be fine."

The omega could not respond with words and felt like he had just been more than a little exposed. But he knew that the doctor was a trustworthy confidant and would not let anything said in this room leave. He was still embarrassed by the whole situation, but it soon eased away into a normal routine of standard health questions for both physical and mental health before everything was finished and Andrew found himself heading down the familiar stairs with a slight spring in his step.

Turning right, the omega headed down the street to a vending machine that was filled with his favourite brand of milk and pressed the buttons for a bottle of strawberry and cream. It was very sweet but always the nicest pick me up after any therapy session and had become a welcomed treat for the omega.

Just as he was picking the bottle up out of the slot, Andrew nearly jumped out of his skin when an alpha approached him unexpectedly and said, "Hey, little one." There was an instantly recognisable tea tree scent that caused a blush to cross Andrew's cheeks.

Tristan smiled at him charmingly, leaning almost like a model against the wall, in an outfit which had to be designed by Daniel. Slick fitted jeans that were not too tight but made an impression with their dark stone-washed texture; a blue ruffle shirt with a few buttons left teasingly open at the top; and a thin, black waistcoat. The alpha's hair had been styled neatly up and back, exposing his forehead a little and allowing those intensely dark blue eyes to bore deeply into the omega's which sent a shiver down Andrew's spine.

In fact, he felt more like melting into a puddle than he normally did with the heat of the midmorning sun, and for a second he couldn't even think how he should appropriately react to the sight of Tristan standing there like that.

Thankfully, the cool and very calm Tristan just smiled and moved across to the shy, rather awkwardly tall omega and gently cupped the side of his face with his hand. "Do you come here often, my little one?" he teased in the cheesiest of pick-up lines. Irritatingly, it worked on Andrew perfectly.

Nine

Walking and Talking

Tristan gently ran his thumbs across Andrew's face when the omega did not move for the better part of thirty seconds. "Did I shock you that much, my little one?"

"A... little," Andrew admitted, blushing and feeling like a complete idiot the second he said it because he was sure that he was acting like a schoolgirl with her first crush. It was completely embarrassing.

However, Tristan just giggled and cooed unashamedly, pinching both of Andrew's cheeks together like he was a little cub. "You are just too cute, you know that? You ruin my attempts to be all cool 'cause I just want to squish your cheeks together so much."

"Tristan!" Andrew had turned bright red and tried to pull away from the face squishing because it was actually starting to hurt a little bit. "You're embarrassing. People can see us!"

"So? I like you when you're being cute, there's no law against that," Tristan said, looping his arm around Andrew's middle and smiled that huge smile up towards the other. That smile did things to the omega that he never wanted to admit to. "You are the cutest omega ever and I don't care if anyone stands and gawps at us. I want the world to know that you're mine and that you are completely adorable."

A side-eyed glare came his way as Andrew tried to start walking, hoping that the tittering of a group of high school girls nearby weren't what he thought they were, or that the curious stares of an elderly beta couple who were doing their shopping were not judging him for the public display of affection. He could almost see the look in the alpha's eyes across the street, his nose slightly upturned at the idea that he would allow someone to treat him that way so publicly and thanks to his twitching ears, Andrew heard the man mutter, "Weak alpha, letting his omega prance around like some idiot."

Blinking in surprise, Andrew glanced down at Tristan wondering how on earth anyone could genuinely think that he was the omega in the relationship only to find himself pulling back as something was shoved directly under his nose. A sneeze followed not five seconds afterwards, followed by seven more in quick succession.

Tristan produced a handkerchief and offered it to Andrew. "Bless you, are you okay?"

"Yes," Andrew said and then promptly sneezed again, twitching his nose in irritation before looking at Tristan. The alpha was holding a single stemmed flower which was wrapped up in clear plastic with little, white hearts and butterflies on it. "What's that for?"

"Oh this?" Tristan said, smiling stupidly and acting shy for a second. "Well I couldn't really take you out on a date without some kind of gift, could I? So, I bought you this."

The flower had a very soft, purple colouring and had lovely little white patches on it. For a second Andrew was torn between feeling as though he was dancing somewhere on the clouds to being utterly dismayed because clearly his Tristan had not spoken to Daniel first about what type of gift he should get Andrew for this sort of situation.

Before he could explain however, he sneezed again quite loudly and Tristan stepped closer with the flower and another handkerchief, that was dotted with yellow spots. "Are you sure you're okay, Andrew? You've not caught a cold or something have you?"

Andrew shook his head, ears drooping ever so slightly, "No... it's the... achoo... flower!"

"Huh?" Tristan looked down at the flower and then back towards Andrew in confusion for a few seconds before his black ears perked up as realisation struck. "You're allergic to flowers?"

"Only certain ones," Andrew managed to thankfully catch the sneeze that was threatening to explode out of his nose with the handkerchief this time and he smiled apologetically towards Tristan. "I love gladioli but they bring me out in a sneezing fit."

"Oh," Tristan pouted adorably. "Well... sorry."

Andrew couldn't help but shake his head, feeling a light tug of a smile on his face. "It's fine, you didn't know."

"Hmm, I think there's a flower stall just down here so I can always just give it to them and they can make a little extra." Tristan smiled, catching hold of Andrew's hand to start tugging him down towards the main street with a smile. "Not exactly the way I planned to start our date but I guess it could have been worse."

A resounding sneeze came from Andrew which pretty much proved that point and Tristan did honestly feel guilty about being the accidental cause of it all. He stopped at the flower stall to hand the flower over and tell the lady to sell it on for him because he had made a slight mistake and then he had promptly gone and bought a bottle of water and a small, rabbit-shaped candy floss for Andrew to make up for it.

Andrew had opted to sit on a wall nearby and seemed to be ducking his head down a fair bit. Tristan frowned and hurried back, realizing that his omega was looking as though he was about to pass out. "Did you bring a hat or anything with you today, Andrew? You really don't look that great.

Andrew shook his head, accepting the water and handing the handkerchief back to Tristan who folded it neatly and placed it in his pocket. "I'm not usually picked up and taken somewhere after my appointments," he admitted a little shyly. "Normally I go home and nest."

Tristan hummed, "Well if you want we can go do that instead. If I'm allowed in your nest, of course, 'cause that's totally up to you." The alpha looked somewhat panicked but he smiled softly to hide his discomfort. "Or if there's something else you want to do then we can go with that too. I need to make up for this being the worst date ever, right?"

There was a pause as Andrew took a gulp out of the water bottle before the words finally registered with the omega. "Wait. What?"

There came a chuckle from the smaller alpha. "We're on a date Andrew."

"But... what... you... I... Erm..." Andrew felt the flush return to his face almost ten times worse than before. Typically he had decided to wear a red jumper today as well so it was even more hideous to be blushing this much in public. "You shouldn't..." the omega floundered because he just did not know what to say or how to react in this situation. It was so flustering and embarrassing and Tristan was so perfect but... the omega did not realise that he was blurting all of these intrusive thoughts out into the open air like this.

"Hey, hey it's okay my little one," Tristan said softly, stepping forward to run his fingers over the edge of Andrew's ears, something which he had found out a long time ago was soothing and could relax the younger wolf down in a matter of seconds. "You're here with me. You're safe and I'm taking you out on a date because I promised you that I would yesterday, remember?"

Andrew did remember that promise but it still seemed to be a little on the surreal side. Lightly he sighed and looked up towards Tristan's eyes, trying to read into them. "You said…"

"That I would take you to your favourite cat-sith cafe." Tristan smiled in return. "And that's what we're doing. Practically anyone would call it a date, so why not give it the correct term from the start?"

Looking down at the ground, Andrew scuffed his feet. "I'm sorry."

"What for?" Tristan asked softly.

Andrew shook his head. "I'm like this all the time Tristan. I just… freak and lose confidence all the time. You'll get sick of that eventually."

"No, I won't," came the stubborn reply, "not in a million years."

The omega wanted to yell in frustration but he didn't. Instead his mouth opened and closed several times as he tried to form the words which he hoped would explain himself somehow to the other. He needed to make the alpha see that he was probably better not wasting his time on him when they were doomed to failure because Andrew couldn't get his act together and stop freaking out. He tried, he really did try, but his attacks of fear and anxiety were always going to be a big problem and no alpha deserved having to deal with an emotionally unstable omega who would cause problems somewhere along the line because he just couldn't keep up with the world.

Taking a deep breath to try and push Tristan away verbally, Andrew was shocked to silence instead when he found Tristan's lips on his. The kiss was long, soft and gentle and after a few mere seconds Andrew found himself relaxing, the tension in his body receding and a breath of relief escaped from his lips as Tristan pulled back so that he could look at the other straight in the eyes and smile.

"Andrew, I'm not here to rekindle an old love affair or be some fairy tale prince who comes in on a white horse and all of that. I came back here for you, because I wanted to come back for you. I know a little about your problems. I know that you still freak out and try to run away and I know that you'll push me away. Or you'll try to because you can't trust anyone. Or you think you can't because of what happened to you all those years ago."

Slowly Tristan raised his hand up, the one that still held the bite mark which Andrew had made on that horrible night and made sure that Andrew was looking directly at it. "But I also know that you chose me to be your rock, to be someone you could have confidence in on that night. Whilst you were terrified and completely out of your mind, the omega in you sought out the protection that it wanted and I'm still here for you. I'm not going to say that it's going to be an easy path, because I'm not that stupid and I'm certainly not here to win any awards as the world's best alpha or anything like that. But I will be there for you Andrew. Through everything. Through the frustration, through the anger, through the worst times and through the best times, because if there was one thing I learnt in the city whilst I was there, it was that life is not always as it appears. There are so many ways that we can work this through together."

Staring straight into Tristan's eyes, Andrew did the first thing that both his head and heart agreed on in that second.

He flung his arms tightly around Tristan and held onto his guardian, his protector, to the wolf that would undoubtedly be the reason why he continued to live in this ever-changing world. He found that there were no tears to shed, no unnecessary babbling of words, just a soft beating sound which took him a good minute or two to recognise as his own heartbeat matching Tristan's perfectly.

Tristan gently kissed the tips of his ears. "There, my little one, you know that you'll always be safe with me. Regardless of what happens."

Slowly pulling back, Andrew managed a weak smile towards Tristan. "I still think that you're far too good for me."

"According to your elder brother, I'm possibly the most idiotic and stupid thing that ever happened to you," came the cheeky reply before Tristan leant forward to steal another quick kiss from the omega. "Now come on, I've got a really great place lined up for us and if we don't hurry we're going to have to queue and in this heat I really don't think that's a good idea for you."

Offering his hand again, Tristan was overjoyed when Andrew took it and gently he tugged the other along so that they could start down the street. His black tail wagged happily back and forth, unable to hide his glee at the sweet motion. He was thankful that whilst his omega had been at the appointment he had had the time to find out exactly where the café he wanted to take Andrew to was and how to get there so that he didn't end up lost.

There was no talk between them for a few minutes, mainly because Andrew was eating the sweet treat that he had been given and was unknowingly getting sugar everywhere, but Tristan thought it was just too adorable to mention so didn't bother. Instead he hummed happily as they walked along the streets, occasionally glancing into shop windows but never allowing himself to be distracted for too long.

"Doesn't it bother you?" Andrew asked quietly once he had finished the treat.

"What?" Tristan asked, tearing his eyes away from a display of plushies in a crane game. He knew if he started playing that then they would have no money for the café.

Andrew blinked, frowning at his partner. "There's been at least five or more wolves in the last few minutes who have mistaken you for an omega."

"Really?" Tristan blinked, turning to look up at Andrew and forgetting his mental calculation on how likely he was to win one of the cute ducks out of the claw machine.

Nodding in response, Andrew couldn't help but frown when Tristan burst out laughing and picked up his pace again. "Oh boy, I guess I really don't act like an alpha then."

"Huh?" Andrew could only respond with confusion, not understanding the other's light-hearted attitude to the situation.

"In the city, I was always being mistaken for an omega," Tristan replied with a grin. "Even in university when I was assigned to the alpha dorms everyone thought there had been a mistake until I roundhouse kicked one of the more persistent alphas into the wall and sent two of the seniors running off with their tails between their legs after I growled at them."

A blink was his response. "You did that?"

"Yeah, didn't I tell you in my letters? Oh no, I didn't actually cause I was too busy gushing about my friend Chester at the time." Tristan grinned. "You'll like him if he ever comes to visit."

"You said that he's a virus," Andrew replied with a tiny pout on his lips.

"A happy virus," Tristan replied while chuckling fondly. "Seriously, he's just got this really happy personality that is annoying but also infectious as anything you can imagine. But he's also the most kind and reliable guy that I've ever met in my entire life. Well when he's not flirting with everything going but he learnt his lesson about that. I hope he gets a job over this side of the tracks. Then you can meet him, 'cause he seriously adored your pictures and even asked to buy a couple from me."

Andrew looked shocked at that comment. "No he did not."

"He did, honestly," Tristan said with a grin, the smile reaching his eyes. "He went through a phase of trying to steal my post so that he could get your artwork before I got a chance to. He's a big goofball and an idiot but so lovely."

Andrew snorted. "I think his alpha will have a hell of a time with him."

"Maybe," Tristan grinned. "He's a beta himself. Though honestly, he could just be very good at hiding it too. Except that time he tried to bear hug me to death, the big git."

"There's an alpha more omega-like than you?" Andrew stated in a deadpan manner.

"Hey! That's mean," Tristan said, lightly flicking his fingers towards Andrew before suddenly brightening when he heard Andrew laughing a little at him. It was only soft and half-hidden because the other was ducking his head and Tristan could not resist the opportunity to hug the tall omega with a happy coo. "There's my little trouble maker, I knew it wouldn't be long before you came back, Andy."

"Oh, stop it," Andrew snapped with no real heat to his words, pushing Tristan back and blushing. "You're being silly."

"So are you," Tristan grinned happily in return, silently amazed that they had been able to fall back into their old, childish ways without so much as a pause of awkwardness between them. It was nice.

Andrew hummed and then flicked his white ears. "What did you mean about Chester getting a job on this side of the rails?"

"Oh yeah, he got himself a job on the OD circuit," Tristan said without much thought behind it.

"The OD?" Andrew asked, sounding puzzled.

"Oh, the Omega Date programme." Tristan realised that Andrew probably knew very little about that service. "It's for omegas who don't have mates and don't want a total stranger to help them through the heat or go through it alone."

"It's a dating thing then?" Andrew asked, not quite getting why anyone would want to sign up to anything like that.

Tristan shook his head. "Not quite. There are dates involved but it's more of a matchmaking service really. Omegas can apply to the service so that when their heat is due they can be paired with a suitable alpha who will take them through their heat and ensure that they are well looked after the whole time. It's completely legal and to even be considered you have to be practically of idol status. Everything is checked out on both parties beforehand so it's perfectly safe and very popular."

"And your friend works for them?" Andrew asked, wondering just how that could be seen as a career.

Tristan replied with a nod. "Yeah, he got a spot confirmed during his last year of university as long as he passed with flying colours and since he came second in the year, he was pretty much in the training course before we had a chance to celebrate."

For a few seconds Andrew was quiet, mulling over the words that the other had said and then he tilted his head towards Tristan. "I don't get the point of that service."

"Me either to be truthful," Tristan replied with a bright smile as he turned down a side street and carefully dodged a group of happy children on their bikes. "But there again, we've not exactly grown up the same as many others so I suppose that's what could be the difference."

Nodding again, Andrew took a gulp of his water before realizing that he had completely forgotten about the milk that he had bought earlier. He resolved to just save it as a treat for later. Blinking, he turned to ask Tristan a question only to find himself mentally pausing to admire the alpha some more. In some ways, it was perfectly fine that Tristan was smaller than him, because it gave Andrew an excuse to be gazing at the other and not be noticed unless Tristan was also looking up. He admired the other's side profile, from the tips of his black ears, down his lovely sloping nose to a pair of lips that were just made exclusively for kissing and a long neck that looked to be quite biteable.

Realising where his thoughts were taking him, Andrew straightened, blushed and turned to look away. He prayed that he had not been caught doing something so silly and embarrassing. He was really trying not to be some ditzy high school girl from the teen dramas that he liked to indulge in from time to time.

He flicked his ears ever so slightly, and then turned to Tristan with a questioning look. "Why are you humming 'Summer Puppy Love'?"

Tristan stopped humming, mainly because he was a little ashamed of getting caught, and looked guilty for a few seconds. "I'm... I just... I really like that song?" Lightly the alpha shrugged, looking a little bashful. "I know it's cheesy and aimed at kids but..."

"You still watch those films?" Andrew asked carefully, remembering the rainy nights when he couldn't sleep and Tristan would come over to his house with a bunch of blankets and they would make a fort out of all of them. Then they would snuggle up on the biggest pile of pillows to watch the 'High Paw Musical' films back to back. Nine times out of ten they would be asleep straight after their favourite song of 'Summer Puppy Love' but there were times when they managed to watch all four two-hour-long films without finding the need to fall asleep until long after the sun had risen.

A knowing smile crossed Tristan's face. "I heard that they're bringing out a fifth film in a couple of weeks. Do you want me to get us tickets for it?"

Blushing madly once again, Andrew looked down but nodded instead of spurting out a thousand and one reasons why the other shouldn't be buying him the tickets for that silly film. He knew very well that it would be silly, dopey and probably a reboot or a continuation with older actors that may or may not work but there was just something about them all that Andrew still enjoyed to this day. When he had first heard about the film coming out he had been so sad because he knew that Daniel would kill him if he had to sit through another one and he really couldn't imagine Viola being up for it either. In fact, Viola had always blamed her elder cousin for her extreme dislike of the films because of the number of times that she had been forced to sit through them.

Plus, Andrew knew that regardless of what he actually said, Tristan was likely to go and buy him the tickets and drag him to the pictures to see them anyway. "If you can though, try and get a private box."

"A private box?" Tristan asked, raising his eyebrows slightly.

Andrew nodded. "Yeah, it stops me freaking out."

"Oh, if an unknown alpha sits next to you?" Tristan guessed correctly and nodded, squeezing Andrew's hand. "That makes perfect sense. Though I think I'll be about the only alpha in the place, it's not typically our kind of film."

A light chuckle escaped from Andrew's lips for a second, before he hid it with a drink of water. "I know. Daniel was mad at me for a week when I forced him to take me to the fourth one."

"That was because he had to tell people that he wasn't dating his little brother," Tristan replied, grinning as he accepted a drink from the bottle before he chuckled. "He would never admit to having a soft spot for that series."

"Gege hates 'High Paw Musical'," Andrew said, shaking his head from side to side and vaguely wondering if his sudden talkativeness was purely being caused by Tristan or his hormones playing havoc with him. "He would always groan and grumble about having to be forced to watch them and made me sit through an action film to make up for the 'cinema trip of hell' as he called it."

Gently Tristan licked his lips. "Don't tell him that I told you but Daniel asked me to get him a limited edition stationery pack for the fourth one just for him."

"What?" Andrew asked, staring at Tristan. "He did not."

"Oh, he did." Tristan grinned cheekily. "He asked me to get one for you and one for that omega he had his eye on a couple of years ago but they were just the normal releases. The limited edition with the full stationery set, phone charms, cast-signed photo and the special gift he ordered for himself."

Andrew blinked. "I've never seen that."

"It'll be hidden somewhere or he'll have it in his flat so that you can't find it." Tristan continued grinning. "Sometimes it's a bit of a curse being an alpha."

"Why?" Andrew asked, genuinely intrigued.

"Cause we're not supposed to like cute things or do soppy stuff and all of that jazz even though we all know that most omegas absolutely love it. If we were to get involved with it all then we'd have so many potential partners that it would be quite the fun time," Tristan replied with a slight blush. "Though like I said before, I never once cared about it and had plenty of omega friends who were all convinced that I was an omega. Even my beta friends thought I was."

Andrew snorted. "Are you sure you didn't just deliberately act like one to keep yourself free?"

"Ohhh, do I detect a little bit of jealousy there?" Tristan teased back, cooing when he saw the shy, sweet look of someone who had just been completely caught out on his omega's face. "Don't look so cute otherwise I'll just squish your face some more."

Tristan placed a sweet little kiss on the tip of Andrew's nose, before starting to speak suspiciously rhythmically. "Plus, like I said before, and I'll probably say a million more times before you actually believe me, my little one, you are my only one and..."

"No!" Andrew said, pulling back and taking a few steps away, recognising the start of the song and not wanting it to be sung at him in public because it would make him go gooey and soft. "You are not singing that song to me right now!"

"Aww but Andy!" Tristan called, chasing after the other. "You know you love it!"

"Tristan!" Andrew whined, now looking completely embarrassed. "You're making a scene!"

"Of course I am, but I'm totally allowed to," Tristan replied, grinning from ear to ear before gently catching hold of Andrew's hand and tugging him off down another street. "Okay, I'll stop. It's not my fault that you're so cute and adorable."

Whining once again, Andrew began to tell Tristan to stop because even though he was enjoying the attention he was sure that at some point it was going to stop being fun. Although he really wished that it would never come to that point. However, before he could get the words to form properly, his eyes fell on something very cute and very cherry-red.

In fact, it was a dust-grey rabbit in a white and gold hanfu, a beautiful, long dress with the skirt coming up above the chest. The shoulders were covered with a bright cherry-red overcoat that was lined with snow-white fluff. The ears were adorned with sparkly flower stones and jade representations of little flowers. Dusty was the Star Rabbit from 'Space Buddiez', guardian of fun, youth and laughter who enjoyed making yummy food and brightening up everyone's day by cleaning out all the nasty dust bunnies. There was a sign next to Dusty that read, 'Café this way', with an arrow pointing down the street.

Andrew smiled softly at the figure and then reached out to pet her as he always typically did with anything that was related to 'Space Buddiez' and was only brought out of his little trance when there came the click of a camera. He turned and playfully pouted towards Tristan, before his eyes flicked up the small set of stairs that his partner was already standing on with a knowing grin.

"Come on, Andrew," Tristan said, offering his hand towards the other for the fifth time in the past half hour. "Let's go on our date, huh?"

Blinking like a child, Andrew stared at Tristan like he was completely insane before looking up the steps to what could only be the Dusty Café and then back towards Tristan with a distinct look of confusion in his eyes. He did this several more times, clearly not able to comprehend what was going on and mentally debating over whether he should turn tail and run, or rush up the stairs ahead of Tristan to confirm that this was real. "I thought you said that we were going to the cat-sith café?" he asked in a shy, stammering manner. Almost as if he didn't believe that Tristan would actually step up and get him a spot in the Dusty Café as it was an exclusive pop up that was only around for a limited time and even getting a reservation was next to impossible.

Grinning with all the affection he could muster, Tristan let out a chuckle and simply replied, "Surprise."

Then the alpha moved down the few steps that he had climbed, took a firm hold of Andrew's hand and gave him a firm tug until they were standing in the courtyard outside the very pink and purple café where the door jangled open as a happy group of school cubs walked out, their ears adorned with cute, sparkly flowers and stars that they had bought from the store inside. Tristan could not help but smile brightly as he headed in, feeling Andrew's grip on his hand tighten just ever so slightly.

"Reservation for Tristan and special guest," he said politely to the beta who was greeting guests and they were led to a small table towards the back of the café which had bright pink chairs, an adorable, white, lace table cloth set with purple condiments and a small, bright pink, thankfully artificial, rose which was sprinkled with lots of sparkling glitter.

Andrew sat down opposite him, looking around in wonder as if he didn't know where to look first and Tristan could only smile brightly at the fact that he had made his mate so happy. He nearly jumped out of his skin when Andrew leaned forward to press a light kiss to his lips before pulling back with a soft, "Thank you."

Tristan smiled back even more brightly than he had been before. "You're welcome. I think you're going to enjoy this date way more than I am."

For once Andrew nodded, allowing his usual, small smile to become just a little wider than it had been in a long while and Tristan was glad to have left the photo app open on his phone so that he could snatch the shot before it was gone. He'd do anything and everything to make Andrew happy and this was a good start in his books. A very good start.

Ten

Of Star Rabbits

Lining up the shot on his phone, Tristan grinned as he managed to capture another photo of his beloved omega happily playing with a large Dusty Rabbit doll and looking completely besotted. It was the first time in a long while that the alpha remembered seeing Andrew looking anywhere near as content and happy as he did now, and it made him want to let out several happy little grumbles himself. He had made his omega happy and his inner wolf was practically running circles in head with a mad case of the zoomies, which was his way of expressing that he was having a lot of fun.

If the omega noticed that he was being continuously photographed, Andrew did not show any signs of distress which was a relief. His white ears were perked up and his tail kept swishing back and forth in a happy motion, whilst his sweet scent of gingerbread brought out joyous memories of holidays and snuggling up together on long winter nights.

It had been an almost instinctive thing for Tristan, as they entered the moon-rabbit-themed café, to make a grab for one of the larger dolls from a basket at the counter and give it to his omega. A confused and worried look had been his reply until Tristan practically thrust the doll into Andrew's face and made it dance back and forth with a half-forgotten, little tune spilling from his lips that he hoped would cheer Andrew up. He recalled how he would do this when the omega would want to hide away, buried in his nest or in the darkest corner of the cupboard or wherever else he had found to hide himself away, and would refuse to come out unless Tristan used this specific method. The alpha worried for a few seconds that this may be triggering the omega opposite him but it turned out that he did not have to worry.

Andrew had taken the doll, blushing madly, and was completely fascinated with the toy. Pressing her nose, playing with her ears and giving her a hug every few seconds in the most adorable fashion. The omega was literally acting as though he had been given the one present that he had always wanted and Tristan was happy that he could provide it for his omega. His own tail wagged at the thought that he had provided again and that maybe this was one of the presents that Andrew had always wanted but never dared to ask for. He made a mental note to buy Andrew a Dusty Star Rabbit doll on the way out to take home.

Another click of his phone captured yet another picture of Andrew playing with the doll but this time a large hand reached out to shyly push the device away. "Why do you keep doing that?"

"Doing what?" Tristan asked, already busy saving the image to his gallery because he knew that Andrew would try to delete it if he got half a chance.

Andrew sighed. "Taking pictures of me. You should have more than enough by now."

"I'll never have enough of you, Andrew." Tristan grinned brightly towards the other. "Don't worry, I'll stop for now." It was easy to smell the slight whiff of distress that was coming from his omega and he really didn't want the date to go badly.

Andrew had a puzzled look on his face. "Why do you take them?"

"Because I want to," Tristan shrugged in reply, still smiling. "And because you looked so happy and cute playing with Dusty here that I just wanted to capture the moment."

"But why?" Andrew asked and Tristan mentally reminded himself not to get frustrated at this game of a million questions. He knew that this was all connected to everything that had happened in the past and that Andrew was in his own self-destructive cycle of constantly questioning everything that was said to him. Some days Tristan wished that he could just reverse time and go back and beat the living snot out of the monster who would try and hurt the precious young man in front of him. Even if it was impossible.

Still, he knew that he had to answer Andrew's question or else the date would just turn into a sour mess. "Because I like having photos of you and it makes me happy. When I start work and can't be with you every day, I'll be able to look at those photos on my break and see you and feel better in myself because I know that I can make you happy. That means the world to me."

There was a pause for a few awkward seconds before a shy blush crossed Andrew's face.

"Do you have to be so cheesy?" Andrew asked, hiding his face in the Dusty plush toy which just prompted Tristan to take another photo because it was too cute of a scene not to. Andrew, of course, glared at him, but with no real heat in his eyes.

Tristan grinned right back towards the omega, his own eyes reflecting nothing but the love he clearly held for the other. "You like it when I'm being cheesy."

"You're..." Andrew knew that the word should be 'irritating' or even 'infuriating' but the omega could not bring himself to say it. In his eyes neither of those words described Tristan. He really was the brightest light in the darkness and even though he was sure that he would get burned at some point, Andrew couldn't help but rush towards him with every ounce of his mind, body and soul. He sighed and played with the doll in his hands, pouting a little though it was clear that he was trying desperately not to laugh.

Tristan just continued to smile brightly like the sun and reached across to pet the omega's white ears. "I know. But you still like it. Ohhh, I didn't know that your ears were still silky smooth. That's so cute and perfect."

"They're not," Andrew shot back childishly, flicking his pure white ear out of Tristan's reach for a second before groaning when he remembered that the other was now an adult and could easily pet his ears without much hassle. This was then proven by the fact that Tristan merely reached across the space to start petting them again. Andrew tried to put on a pout as he always claimed to not be one for ear-petting, even if it was clear to everyone that he absolutely adored it, and then flattened his ears down, in the hopes that Tristan would give up. "Stop that."

"Why?" Tristan asked, still petting the ears despite being told not to.

Andrew sent him a pleading look, hoping that the other would get the general idea and just let go of his ear, but Tristan instead flicked his eyes over to a corner where another couple sat. Two young girls, a beta and an alpha were staring at each other with sparkling eyes and the alpha was petting the beta's ears with a soft smile on her face. Andrew found it within himself to snort. "They're sixteen and cute, we are not."

"No one knows our age," Tristan countered, suddenly appearing on Andrew's side of the table with his chair so that he could wrap his arm securely around the omega and continued to pet his silken ears. "And we do look cute together."

Another whine escaped from Andrew but he stopped short of spluttering out any complaints when the waitress arrived with an order. Tristan must have made it whilst he was distracted by the doll. The order contained two strawberry ice coffees; a bright pink cake slice; and a selection of cookies. Andrew blushed when the waitress smiled politely at them and said that there was a small couple section upstairs if they wanted to take a selfie together after their meal and Tristan nodded his thanks as she left the table.

"See," Tristan said smugly, picking up a cookie to bring it towards Andrew's lips. "Told you so."

Andrew pouted but accepted the cookie regardless because he had been caught out. He still didn't get why anyone would think that they were a cute couple, however. It was strange for certain or even on some levels weird because the one who was supposed to be small was tall and the one supposed to be tall was small. However Andrew rather liked the fact that Tristan was small, as it just fit him well and he still gave the best hugs and part of the omega was interested to discover what it would be like to spoon with the alpha at some point.

He flushed a bright red at that thought and quickly made a grab for the strawberry iced coffee to down as much of it as he could in one go. Tristan gave him a slightly confused look, but Andrew rapidly shook his head and looked so awkward that the alpha just let him be. It was always a better idea to not push too far and keep things on an even keel.

The rest of the hour they spent in the café was relatively silent, mainly because Andrew gave up on fighting the need to push Tristan away and instead allowed himself to enjoy the sensation of being cuddled up to his mate, basking in his familiar tea tree scent and just allowing himself to be looked after. It had been an awfully long time since he had last indulged in this sort of treatment and it felt good to be able to do so. Tristan fed him cookies and cake, smiling gleefully in that happy alpha way that was adorable and dopey at the same time.

"Cookie for your thoughts," Tristan asked in a quiet, little whisper, his lips just brushing over the sensitive sections of his ears after some time in companionable silence.

"I want to stay feeling safe like this," Andrew replied without evening pausing to stop and think about what he was saying. "I... really... really like... this... this... feeling."

Pride swelled up in Tristan's heart as he let out a contented little grumble, his wolf showing its pleasure at those words. The alpha was bristling with pride, strutting around with its nose stuck up in the air because his mate felt safe around him. He was protecting, he was providing and that was what a great alpha was supposed to do. He would forever strive to be the only alpha for Andrew, to be the one who would care for him and look after him throughout all the troubles that could come around in the next few months or years and he would never falter.

Tristan wanted to be Andrew's world. He wanted to make Andrew smile all of the time and act like a happy omega who could be around all sorts of different people, who was no longer afraid of the past, of his shadow and of the cubs that he so clearly wanted to be with. Tristan would forever be Andrew's alpha, his guardian who would make sure that everything turned out to be exactly what they each wanted it to be.

The words did not need to be spoken, they were already engraved upon their hearts by the actions that had brought them together, no matter how dark and depressing that time had been. Tristan kissed the top of Andrew's head again as he fed him the cookie. "Good," was all he said on the matter and that was more than enough for now.

Once their treats were finished, Tristan paid without much of an argument from Andrew. The omega figured that regardless of what he said there was no way his alpha was going to allow him to pay for the date. The next one would be on Andrew, the omega decided, even if he would have to do some serious research on where to take the alpha because this little surprise was going to take some beating. Plus, if the omega was actually truthful with himself, it was nice to be spoiled by an alpha, one that he didn't automatically presume wanted something in return for this. There had been a few cases of this in the past where young alphas had tried to treat him as part of his therapy but it generally ended in disaster. There was one alpha who had proven to be genuinely honest and kind with him, as he too already had a mate from a young age and was no threat. However, there had only been a couple of meetings between them and things had fizzled out naturally.

Tristan tugged Andrew upstairs to see the little flat that was made exclusively for Dusty, and Andrew practically melted with how cute it all was. It was like walking into a perfect little princess room with everything set out exactly how it should be and it was all adorable. There were little cupboards that held plates, cups and saucers which all matched up perfectly, a table with a cosmic pink and purple flower that was set up in a vase and an old-fashioned oven with a cozy log fire burning in it. The living room was all tiny little white sofas with a large TV and a bookshelf filled with a selection of books that covered topics of family, friends, adventures and finding oneself through cleaning martial arts. There was a burrow-style bedroom with a huge, fluffy nest made out of all sorts of materials, gathered from around the solar system yet all equally important and meaningful in one way or another.

Andrew sat down on the stool that was provided and let out a happy sigh, his own Dusty Rabbit doll in his lap whilst his eyes glistened beautifully with unshed tears. Tristan crouched down next to him with a matching smile before wrapping his arms lightly around the taller omega, "I forgot how much you like Dusty."

"You once emptied out a crane game machine filled with the dolls for me." Andrew smiled with softness and reverence. "And then spent the next year sending me one every month because you couldn't send them all at once."

Tristan laughed. "Yeah, my mother went ballistic at me for that. But it was totally worth it, your face was adorable." Realizing what he had said aloud, Tristan blushed a little as he looked up towards Andrew, rubbing the back of his neck quietly. "Daniel acted a little as my spy and would take photos of you getting your parcels and send them to me."

Staring at the now-blushing alpha, Andrew didn't know if he should be flattered, worried, embarrassed or ecstatic right now because the very idea of Daniel being involved in something like that for him was just an amazing thought. Whilst he knew his elder brother would practically do anything to ensure that he was happy, loved and looked after, it was becoming clear that Andrew did not know half of the extent of what Daniel had done. He would give his brother the biggest hug when he next saw him as well as a thank you, even if it wouldn't begin to cover the cost of what had been gifted to him through the years.

It was even more amazing that Tristan was prepared to put up with everything that Andrew had put him through and a stab of guilt went through his heart. Instead of pulling away from the other and trying to escape however, Andrew did something which he hadn't done in a long while. He turned around on the stool and wrapped his arms tightly around Tristan, burying his face into the crook of the other's neck so that he could inhale the deep scent of tea tree which would forever calm and soothe him. "I'm sorry, Tristan," he whispered quietly. "I'm so sorry."

"What for, my little omega?" Tristan asked, gently flicking his ears though he naturally returned the hug and started to stroke lazy circles on the others broad back.

Andrew gulped, "You've always been so good to me, and I've barely returned anything to you."

Tristan sighed gently, before lightly nipping at Andrew's ears to get the omega to look at him. "Andrew, you've returned more to me than you know."

"But," Andrew started before a finger was placed on his lips and their eyes locked together for what felt like the longest moment in the entire world even though it was barely a couple of seconds.

Looking at Andrew right now, with his wide, innocent eyes; beautiful, sharp features; and a gentle nature about him, Tristan couldn't help but sigh a little in contentment. "I couldn't ask for another like you, ever, I wanted to protect you from the very moment that I laid my eyes on you. The fact that you let me, and have waited for me even though it was one of the most painful things in the entire world... That is more than just a return of everything that I shall do for you. Not many would be prepared to wait five years for their mate to come back to them. Many would just find someone else, but you didn't. You remained faithful to me and I to you."

Blinking slowly, Andrew looked down. "Who else could I have trusted with my heart?"

Guessing that was supposed to be a rather damning statement that had come out a little wrong, Tristan gently lifted Andrew's chin and grinned. "Well, let's just say that I'm still working on getting it and go back to having a fluffy first date." Before Andrew could argue, their lips connected in a soft, gentle kiss. Andrew blushed up a storm but giggled heartily all the same before pushing him away, then immediately pulled him back for several more kisses followed by a long cuddling session.

Thankfully no one complained at them, the staff were even having their own little celebrations when they clocked the cute couple and the pair were just allowed to be for the time being.

They did take a photo in the designated couples spot, and just before they left, there came out a huge, mascot-sized Dusty the Rabbit and of course Tristan shoved Andrew towards the character. After a few awkward seconds, Andrew happily hugged the mascot and Tristan got more cute photos of his omega. For a moment he thought that he would have to literally drag Andrew away from the mascot but the omega let go shortly after and hurried to wrap himself around Tristan with a cute blush.

Tristan was quick to snap a silly selfie of them both, ready with a comeback for the inevitable whine from his omega as he said, "Come on, it's time to go."

"Can I take a picture on my phone?," Andrew asked, pouting in that way which would certainly get the alpha to do anything that he wanted.

Tristan sighed happily and complied, only to be caught off guard when the omega turned their positions around, smacked a kiss directly onto his lips, with the toy clamped right between their bodies and somehow caught the moment on his phone camera before heading away with even more of a blush on his face and a stupid half laugh. The alpha was struck dumb for a couple of seconds and then chased after the omega, despite knowing the fact that he would not be shown that photograph no matter how much he whined and pleaded for it.

Catching up with Andrew just a few steps outside the café, Tristan linked his arm around his omega and grinned up towards him. "You're so cute when you're like this, you know?"

Andrew blushed harder. "I'm not cute!"

"Yes," Tristan nuzzled in as much as he could. "You are."

They fell into a happy, little bubble as they walked back towards the main streets and Tristan began wondering where their feet would take them when Andrew piped up. "Hey, I was just thinking..."

"What about?" Tristan asked casually, catching hold of the doll to carry for Andrew as he seemed to be unable to balance it any further and he didn't want it to drop to the floor.

"If we were to ever have a little girl, could we make her room completely Dusty themed?"

Eleven

Feelings

Tristan choked on air as the statement registered in his mind and he stared at Andrew in shock for a few moments. Then he managed to shake his head, step forward and place a pre-emptive calming hand on the omega's arm. "Did you just..."

"What?" Andrew asked, frowning. Then realisation hit and he stiffened up immediately.

Tristan caught hold of the other before he could run away, "It's okay, baby, it's okay. Breathe, you're fine you're okay..."

Shaking his head, Andrew practically began to collapse in on himself in the street and Tristan glanced around in a panic before spotting a nearby bench that was shaded by a large tree and directed Andrew to it. The omega was beginning to hyperventilate, so the alpha quickly shucked off his jacket and put it over Andrew's head. He kept his voice low, steady and calm and let out as much soothing scent of tea tree as he could. "Andrew, Andy, I need you to breathe okay? I need you to just focus on my voice, and breathe. You've said nothing wrong and I'm not upset about it at all."

Andrew shook his head, hating the fact that there were large, fat tears streaming down his face and horrible-sounding sobs coming out of his mouth. He really needed to get it together, to stop acting like an irrational baby over saying something so stupid when he knew that it was something that was perfectly natural to say. He was an omega for Amarok's sake! He was supposed to think of raising children, to make future plans with his mate for everything but he just felt so guilty and terrible for thinking of a future when he was still fucking up his present.

Tristan stared at the sobbing omega in front of him and pulled the jacket a little further over his head in order to hide him further, as he knew that there were no words that he could offer right now, other than repeating the same statements over and over again like a mantra. He instinctively knew that was not what Andrew needed right now.

His little omega needed to cry, needed to get these terrible, negative feelings out of his heart and then have someone there to just hug him afterwards. Of course, he wanted to know why that statement would have caused this reaction from Andrew. He had several guesses as to why he would be freaking out like this but he couldn't be certain which one was plaguing the omega right now. All he could do was wait it out. It was hard - extremely hard - for the alpha to see his precious omega so upset by this. But physical contact was not wanted right now. He knew that much.

It took what felt like an eternity for Andrew to calm down enough so that he could form semi-coherent sentences, but Tristan knew to just smile gently at the other and let him choose what he wanted to say. Or not, it was completely up to the omega at this point because while he knew very well that he had the other's trust, there were some things that would take time to come to the surface and Tristan did not want to push Andrew away. It was a delicate balancing act, one that would take a lot of steps to get right and there would be mistakes made along the way.

In their youth, Tristan had made many mistakes without realising it. So had Daniel and the pair's mother, but in time they had come to learn the best way to soothe and provide so it never became too much of an issue. With the separation for the last few years, Tristan feared that he may have lost his touch or was doing something that would be outdated but so far everything seemed to be on the right track to get the omega to come back to him. He did wave off a couple of curious onlookers however, because the last thing Andrew would want would be to have an audience. He hated to be the centre of attention.

Even if most of the time he fully deserved to be.

After a few long moments of silence, Andrew sniffed loudly and asked a question which he already knew the answer to. He just needed the confirmation for himself more than anything else. "Do you have… a handkerchief?"

Tristan dug into his pockets and produced one, passing it straight up to Andrew with a soft smile. "Always."

"Thanks," Andrew said quietly, before blowing his nose and wiping at his eyes. He looked completely miserable as he rested his hands down in his lap, not offering the handkerchief back because it was soggy with his tears. The omega sighed, feeling completely and totally stupid because he had just wrecked the date which Tristan had planned. All because of his stupid, messed up feelings. It just immediately made him want to cry again.

Why couldn't he just sort himself out? Why was it always such a mess like this? He really couldn't stand it, and he couldn't understand how anyone could put up with him. He was a big cry-baby who freaked out over nothing and put everyone that he cared for and loved into situations that were going to wear them down and make their lives just a little harder. He needed to get it together, needed to stop being such an emotional idiot, but he couldn't find the strength and the courage to do it.

Just when he thought that things were possibly getting a little bit better, he would go and screw it all up again.

Jumping in surprise when the handkerchief touched his skin again, Andrew found his teary vision filled by nothing more than the loving face of Tristan who smiled gently at him, "Do you want me to get you a sugary drink? You're beginning to look a little pale and I don't want to explain to your mother that I let you pass out."

Opening his mouth to say something, Andrew just nodded his response instead and took the handkerchief back from Tristan, guilt plaguing him. But all his beloved, little guardian did was to smile, lift himself up from his uncomfortable position to press a light, little kiss to his forehead and say, "Okay, there's a shop just across the road so I'll be in there and I'll be back in five minutes. If you feel the need to hide further, then there's a small hedge behind here that I think should act as a little den if you want to go wild for a bit."

Nodding automatically, Andrew watched as Tristan walked off and wondered once again if the other was actually real or just a figment of his imagination. Of course, he knew the answer because there would just be no way that his imagination could just create someone like Tristan, but at times he really felt as though he was living in a dream when it came to the kind-hearted alpha. It was so hard to envision anyone who could be so understanding and just able to read him at a glance without being too freaked out by it all. Yet there was Tristan every single time. Letting out a huff, Andrew leaned back on the bench, took the jacket off and allowed his head to painfully bash against the years-old wood of the tree. "You idiot, you fucking idiot," he scolded himself quietly under his breath. "Why can't you just... why? Why does it have to be...?"

Tears began to roll down his cheeks again and Andrew leaned forward, not caring that he was causing a scene and tried to stop the tears by placing his face in his hands. "Stop it, stop it, you're being a fucking idiot and you know it. Why does this have to be all screwed up, why can't I have a life like everyone else? What did I do to deserve this? Why did he... why did he screw everything up? Why can't I just... just..."

Of course, his mutterings went completely unanswered, but Andrew found that for the moment they kept him just a little bit grounded and stopped the natural urge to allow change into his wolf form and go and hide in the hedge that Tristan had mentioned. He had already screwed up this wonderful, silly, cute date with his overly harsh and negative emotions, he didn't need to add going wolf on top of that.

His inner omega would just set off for home, for a nest that was familiar and safe and would not come out again anytime soon. He'd try to bite anyone who got close and that was just the worst possible outcome from all the hard work that Tristan had done in order to surprise him with a date. A date that was perfect in conception and execution and should have had Andrew swooning to be so thought of and cherished. Of course he was in reality, as he loved any attention that Tristan would give him but he was just caught in his own self-deprecating cycle right now and did not know how to break out of it.

"An-ge?" A soft, little voice suddenly broke through his mental degradation and he looked up in surprise.

A little girl was standing a few feet away from him, her hair done into a set of nice, little plaits with her golden ears contrasting nicely with her dark brown hair. She was wearing a soft, little summer dress in a light blue with a white undershirt that practically reached all the way to her fingers. She had matching white tights and blue shoes with little ribbons on them and her smile was bright, cheerful and so innocently wonderful that Andrew for a second felt as though he shouldn't be seeing this girl. "It is you, An-ge!" the little girl cried, suddenly rushing forward to give him a hug. "I knew it was you!"

Startled by the little girl's move, Andrew was confused for a few seconds before looking up to see the girl's mother who was giving a fond and overly dramatic sigh. He recognized her as Mrs. Hugh, one of the parents from the local day care where he worked and his sob-ridden brain finally realized that the little girl in his arms was actually Erica. Gently the girl pulled back, her golden ears fluttering in happiness and she smiled brightly at him. "It's been so long, An-ge, aren't you ever coming back to Hummingbirds?"

"Erica," Mrs. Hugh chided playfully, "don't be so rude."

Andrew shook his head at the woman, wiping away the tears a little harder now and smiling as gently as he could towards the little girl. "It's fine, Mrs. Hugh. It has been a long time since I've been, actually."

It had only been a week, but to a little girl like Erica that would seem to be an age. Erica pouted at him. "When are you coming back, An-ge? Everyone is missing you and Ms. Greg doesn't play the way you do."

A half-laugh escaped from Andrew as he reached out to pet the girl's golden ears. "You have to be nice to Ms. Greg, Erica. She has her troubles too, you know."

"I know but even Chujeon is playing up again because you're not at Hummingbirds." Erica pouted rather dramatically. "And if he plays up then we don't get a good nap time and you know that's a bad thing right, An-ge?"

Hummingbirds was a daycare come school for cubs who had a variety of problems which ranged from a slight OCD disorder to autism, mental health issues, physical health issues, specialty diets and even a few cases of abuse victims who were trying to integrate back into society. His therapist had been the one to introduce Andrew to the service, when the omega was trying to find some kind of employment and whilst Andrew had been unsure of the idea of working that closely with so many cubs, he had quickly become a class favourite and he found that he loved the job so much that once his initial placement had been completed he had asked if he could apply as a full-time member of staff.

Naturally they had snapped him up within seconds and it had been one of the main factors in helping his recovery. It had also partially been the reason why he had started to request seeing the pictures and videos of his own cubs, because he had seen how much happier cubs were when they were with people that they loved and cherished.

Erica was a little, golden wolf who had troubles with epilepsy and an aversion to loud sounds as her ears were rather sensitive. Other than that she was a very sweet, little girl who had been one of the many who had wormed her way into Andrew's protected, little heart and if given the chance he would do anything for her. Right now, he smiled at the girl. "Well you can tell Chujeon that if he doesn't start behaving then he won't get any stories about fairies when I get back."

"When will you be back though, An-ge?" Erica asked, pouting a little more. "You've been gone for an age."

Andrew smiled sadly. "In a few weeks, Erica, I'm meeting with someone very important at the moment and I need time with him."

"Why are you crying?" Erica asked suddenly. One of her traits was that she would abruptly switch topics without realising it. "Did those mean boys come and make you cry again?"

The mean boys were actually a bunch of solicitors that Andrew wanted nothing to do with because he was not ready to deal with anything that related to the man who had destroyed his life. It was one of the few times that the elder omega had had a full breakdown in front of the children at Hummingbirds and he still felt as guilty as hell over it. He knew he had to tell Tristan about that at some point, but it was a conversation for another day when he wasn't as emotional. Or more correctly, when his mother was around to act as an extra barrier to the rage that could build up from even the mention of that individual in any of their presence. Quickly he shook his head and focused his attention back on Erica. "No, that's not it, Erica. It's a grown-up problem that you won't understand yet, sweetie."

"But An-ge is sad and he shouldn't be." Erica continued pouting dramatically. "An-ge is always happy."

"Don't worry, little one," Tristan's voice drifted into the conversation as he reappeared with a couple of bottles of pop and a bag of sweets. "I'll make sure your An-ge is happy before we go home."

Erica blinked at the new arrival, recognizing his status and flicking her ears. "Who are you, mister?" she sassed with a look that suggested she'd kick Tristan in the shin despite being double her size if she didn't like him.

"Erica," her mother scolded lightly. "Be polite. I apologise, sometimes she gets like this."

"It's perfectly fine," Tristan replied, bowing to her as he passed Andrew one of the bottles. "My name is Tristan and I'm Andrew's future mate."

The little girl opened her eyes and mouth wide before she suddenly turned to look at the embarrassed Andrew. "An-ge!" she cried, "You didn't tell us that you had found your prince!"

Looking a little bashful, Andrew ducked his head, "Well... I wasn't sure and..."

"Oh, I'm sorry! Are you two on a date?" Mrs. Hugh asked before catching hold of her daughter's hand. "Come on, Erica, we can't interrupt something so important. Sorry if we've caused you any problems at all."

"It's okay," Andrew said as he took a sip out of his drink. "I've always said that she can come and say hi to me if she spots me in the street."

"Hmm, I guess I'll be getting to know you a little better then, Miss. Erica?" Tristan said gently to the girl who suddenly turned a light shade of pink and hid behind her mother before Mrs. Hugh sighed in amusement and set off to continue doing her shopping with a smile which clearly communicated her unspoken thanks.

Tristan waved at the pair as they departed with a bright smile before turning back to Andrew and sitting down next to him. "Feeling better?"

Nodding a little, Andrew took a long gulp of his pop and nearly jumped when a chocolate bar was placed in his hands. "I don't need this much sugar, Tristan."

"You've cried your eyes out and I know you get exhausted after that," Tristan replied, slipping an arm around Andrew to encourage the other to lay his head on his shoulder. "Since we're a bit far out I thought it best to get some sugar into you and then we can head home."

Humming lightly, Andrew took another swig from his bottle before setting it down. "Sorry for ruining your date."

"You haven't ruined it Andrew," Tristan replied, kissing the tips of his ears once again. "I said I was here for the best and the worst, right? You are not losing me that easily."

The pair fell silent again for a bit, just allowing the sun to play through the leaves to gently caress them as the world flowed around them without a care for their situation. Like there was nothing out of place with them just sitting on a bench, in the middle of town, enjoying the quiet.

It was Andrew who broke the silence first. "Aren't you going to ask?"

"About what?" Tristan replied to the question after he finished taking a drink.

"Well..." Andrew gulped audibly, sinking a little further into Tristan's side.

"Do you want to talk about it?" Tristan asked gently, trailing his fingers through the other's blond hair.

Andrew shook his head and huffed out a sigh. "Eventually."

"Okay, but not right now," Tristan said and then he smiled gently, realizing there was a topic he could cover. "So, tell me, who's Erica?"

Caught off guard by the question, Andrew shifted a little before settling down again and chuckling lightly. "She's one of the girls from Hummingbirds, you know the little job I told you about, in my letters once."

"Oh, you still work there?" Tristan asked, smiling gently now. "That's good to know."

"Yeah, got a full-time job there but took a month off to be with you," Andrew replied, blushing immediately again which seemed to just be a full-time thing with him right now. He took another swig of pop. "When I go back I start my child care qualification, so it's working out good for me."

Tristan smiled and gently kissed the top of Andrew's head. "That's excellent. So proud of you."

For a long while the pair were content to just sit on the bench, Andrew cuddled closely to Tristan's side and found that he did not mind it. Softly he let out a breath through his nose and nuzzled closer, enjoying the scent of the alpha and allowing his innermost turmoil to be calmed by the other's presence. He still felt bad for ruining the date by having a complete freak out but he had to be secretly happy that Tristan wasn't running away from him. There had been loads of people who had tried to be his friend only to make their excuses immediately once they had witnessed just how bad Andrew could get when he was upset. Then again, Tristan had always been the one to stick by him, even when times were tough.

He remembered when they were kids, the first time he had had contact with his mother and elder brother after the incident and he had completely freaked out. Too many emotions had gone through his little body at the time, making him lash out, scream, cry and fight anyone who had wanted to come near him. That was until Tristan appeared, and the small alpha had quite simply barged through the throng of adults who were trying to settle Andrew down and wrapped a protective hug around the frightened omega. He had held on tightly, refusing to let go no matter how much Andrew hit, bit and kicked at him until finally the fright left his body completely. He had flopped in Tristan's hold and allowed himself to be washed with the scent of safety and peace that always came with the other and had relaxed.

Daniel had been in tears, confused as to why another alpha had been able to calm his brother down but had quickly composed himself. It had taken a further three visits for Andrew to stop freaking out and recognise the pair for who they truly were and each time Tristan would be there to help keep him calm. It had been wonderful the first time he had been hugged by Daniel and his mother, when his brain stopped trying to trick him with horrible images of what would happen to them, because he had seen them, but secretly he always preferred Tristan's tea tree scent.

It was practically indescribable to the omega, because it was just everything that made him feel happy and relaxed all rolled into one. It was one of the reasons why he was so careful with everything that Tristan had sent him over the years, wanting nothing more than to just wrap himself in that wonderful smell forever. Now he actually had the other here with him, could wrap himself in the scent whenever he wanted and that was something that just made butterflies run through every last part of his mind, body and soul.

Andrew still felt terrible about ruining the date, and decided to try and make up for it. He looked towards Tristan through his eyelashes, noticing that the alpha appeared to be so content like this and it almost made the blond-haired omega stop for a moment or two but he shook his head and quickly made up his mind. "Tristan?" he asked quietly. "Do you still have some free time today or do you have to go home after this?"

Shaking his head, the black-eared alpha smiled. "Nope, I've got all day to spend with you. Do you have any plans?"

A tiny smile crossed Andrew's face. "Not really. I've got something that I need to do however, I just don't know what you'll think of it."

"I really don't mind," Tristan replied, stroking the white ears with affection, "as long as I'm with you..."

"Stop being cheesy, I don't think I could stomach it," Andrew sighed before pulling himself away from Tristan with a little reluctance and desperately tried to hide a smile.

A chuckle came from Tristan as he stood next to Andrew and reached up to squeeze his cheek. "Sorry, I can't help it when you're so adorable."

Shaking his head as he sighed again, Andrew kept his eye-line low out of nothing more than habit and found that he did not have it in his heart to come up with some kind of retort to that statement. Gently he laced his fingers with Tristan's and started off down the path that would lead him to an all-too-familiar track. It was funny to think that the number of times he had walked down here, he had never once even considered the option of heading to the Dusty Café but put it down to the simple fact that it would look a bit strange to go in by himself. Sure, he was an omega but even so it was a little on the strange side.

Tristan happily began humming that song from 'High Paw Musical' as they walked, enjoying the comfortable silence that could exist between them and Andrew had to admit that he was enjoying it as well. It was something as mundane as just walking along the street, hand in hand with the wolf who was his mate in all but the official claim mark, that felt so precious and lovely. Andrew suddenly began to understand why there were always happy smiles on the faces of the omegas that he saw walking around. This was indeed a nice feeling, one that kept him grounded and made him feel as though life was worthwhile. He guessed that this was what it meant to be happy, to have the other half of your soul with you at all times and he could only hope that he could break through his stupid anxieties to be the perfect mate that Tristan needed and deserved.

He wanted Tristan to say he was proud of him, to be his reliable rock when times got hard and to make it so that the world would be theirs to conquer. Andrew wanted one day to not freak out over the idea that he would have his own cubs and family with Tristan, he didn't even know how he could possibly begin to even explain what he was feeling to Tristan when he said those words. It was certainly something that should not really be uttered on a first date, but realistically they were long past that. But it was still very scary.

However, Tristan would allow him to take all the baby steps he needed. For Andrew, that was the most precious commodity that he had right now.

Twelve

Right by Your Side

They were deep into the shopping district before Tristan stopped humming and glanced around. "I thought you hated shopping?"

"I do," Andrew said, glad that he wasn't turning into a shaking leaf with the number of people around. The omega had a streak of irrational paranoia that he would be stolen away from those who were around him. "But we're not staying in these streets for long."

"Where are we going?" Tristan asked, as Andrew pulled off the main street and started down a long, winding one that had a smaller selection of artisan shops. Tristan couldn't help but be curious as he passed them by, seeing that each one was completely different from the next and all of them had a variety of unique items for sale. There was an alternative fashion shop, followed by a place filled with plants that had grown to resemble mythical creatures. Next along was an old-world trinket place filled with hand-carved ornaments and toys, and then an art gallery that was selling lots of original works.

There was a book shop next that immediately caught Tristan's attention because it looked to be at least three stories high and smelt wonderful. The old book smell was heavy in the air and the alpha indulged his senses just a little bit. It was his second favourite smell in the entire world, the first naturally being the gingerbread scent that came from his mate. His eyes lingered longingly on the heavyset spines and he accidentally tripped over the kerb. Andrew glanced back and then grinned. "Oh, I forgot you liked books."

"There's so many of them," Tristan replied, clearly still enamoured. "I could spend hours in there."

"And you will," Andrew said, squeezing Tristan's hand, "but there's a place that I need to take you to first."

Blinking, Tristan pouted towards his mate but that quickly changed to a smile. "Is that a promise?"

"Yes," Andrew said meekly. "It's just the shop we're going to has a funny closing time so I want to go there before I let you loose in that book shop."

"I should have brought a bigger bag," Tristan lamented playfully as Andrew tugged him past the bookstore. "There'll be a load of books in there that I want."

Lightly rolling his eyes, Andrew sighed. "Well just remember that you're still in your old room. You haven't got a place to set up a library yet."

Tristan stared at Andrew. "How did you know I wanted a library in my house?"

"You always used to have one," Andrew said, looking back towards Tristan. "Whenever we would play house, you always had to have a library to put all of your books in."

The alpha blinked, his ears raising in surprise. "I played house with you?"

"Yes, hundreds of times." Andrew shook his head, ears drooping a little. "Don't you remember the time when we tried to build a library using cardboard boxes and accidentally gave Daniel a bump on the head when the boxes fell over?"

For a second or two, Tristan didn't know how to respond but then he recalled the incident and felt an odd sort of blush cross his face. "Oh yeah, that time. I ended up having to play nursemaid to him for a fortnight afterwards didn't I?"

"You practically volunteered," Andrew replied dryly though he chuckled for a second. "I think my mother still has the photos of you in the apron and headband actually."

Tristan blanched at that, clinging to the omega to silently beg him to never release those photos to anyone which caused a chuckle to appear on Andrew's lips. They quickly settled back into their hand-in-hand walk down the shop fronts until they finally came to a stop in front of one called "The Lost Pencil."

The display of the front of the shop was filled with all sorts of stationery the likes of which Tristan was pretty sure that he had never even seen before. It was original, cute, and had him feeling as though he was a little kid about to go and buy his school supplies for the first time all over again. Each and every last piece was bright, colourful and seemed to match with everything around it whilst being completely different at the same time. The themes ranged from ballerinas, princesses and fairies to knights, superheroes and racing cars. They had all been arranged together by colour, so that it appeared there was a rainbow of stationery in the front of the shop.

Tristan was particularly drawn to a fluffy, grey and white, okami-shaped pencil case but was tugged away by Andrew who had a soft smile on his face. "No."

"What?" Tristan replied, pouting and a little annoyed that he had been caught. "Why?"

"Because I already have that one and all the others in the Yok-Ai line." Andrew replied with a shy, little smile.

A blink passed across Tristan's face. "Oh, really? Who got you them?"

"Leroy," Andrew replied with a smile. "He was the one who found this place and he kept on buying them for me. He thought they were plushies."

"Isn't Leroy Viola's friend?" Tristan asked, trying to recall if that was right or not.

Andrew nodded, "Yeah he is but he was involved in Hummingbirds for a while and attended one of the extra classes with me because he's got... well some problems. So, he's my friend too."

"Oh, that's nice," Tristan nodded. "I take it he's an omega like you and Viola?"

The omega shook his head, his eyes darting over the window display with a curious gaze. "No. He's an alpha."

"An alpha?" Tristan half stammered. "But you..."

"An extremely soft, fluffy, unicorn-obsessed alpha who barely remembers that he is one," Andrew quickly put in with a smile.

"But he's still an alpha," Tristan said, looking a little cross.

Andrew sighed and leaned in close to whisper. "He's got physical problems too."

At the raised eyebrow that he received from his potential mate, Andrew sighed and found two things running through his heart. The first was frustration because he knew that Leroy was completely harmless and wouldn't hurt another living being if he could avoid it. Hell, he had gone into a full crying fit after having to pull a splinter out of one of the cubs at Hummingbirds because the cub had been in so much pain. Although, once it was out and the cub had gone immediately running back to their friends without so much as a care in the world. The other emotion that ran through Andrew's heart was a glowing sense of pride that Tristan really was that protective over him and did not trust the fact that another alpha was near his omega. It caused the most wonderful butterflies to flutter in his stomach and he would have easily blushed if not for the fact that he was trying to quell the potential concern and rage that could come from Tristan.

"Leroy's a soft alpha," Andrew whispered gently to Tristan.

Soft alphas were the type that did not exhibit the normal degree of aggression and territorial claiming when it came to lands or mates. They were just as physically strong, but were far more level-headed in temperament and did not get strong desires when they were in rut. For a while many had thought that Tristan was one, till he nearly ripped some stuck-up jerk a new one because he had been rude to an omega friend.

Tristan lowered his head a little. "Sorry."

"It's no problem," Andrew said with a small smile. "Most people don't believe it when they first hear it either. Come on."

Tristan nodded and followed the omega into the shop. The stationery was so bright and colourful that it was easy to get lost in it all and the designs were fun. There were a few he recognised, mainly being the 'Space Buddiez', 'The Red Force' and the 'Yok-Ai' that his omega had pointed out, though he desperately wanted to buy more of the latter brand as it was clear that Andrew loved them all. But the omega kept on going until they were almost at the back of the shop where there was a whole set of stationery themed around a gingerbread dragon.

Literally a dragon made of gingerbread, with soft-looking, iced details that had a family and a whole little storyline around it. There was a male and a female adult, along with three little dragonets who just looked adorable with their gumdrop decorations. Tristan couldn't help but smile brightly upon making the link, even if he had been very much aware of it before. "Gingerbread Dragon!"

It was Andrew's turn to stare at Tristan with scrutiny. "What?"

"Gingerbread Dragon," Tristan said with a knowing smile. "It's adorable that you use that for the cubs."

Andrew paled considerably, then blushed a bright red and looked down towards the floor with embarrassment. "How do you know about that?"

Gently, Tristan wrapped his arm around Andrew's middle and hugged him. "Yesterday at the party I gave the cubs some cookies which came from the Gingerbread Dragon. They had to tell me because Viola got distracted so I made a mistake and said they were from the fairies. It proved to be quite the conversation I can tell you."

Blinking repeatedly, Andrew sighed. "I... I don't know what to say."

"Just don't worry about it," Tristan said, pressing a little kiss to the side of Andrew's neck. "I think it's adorable and a good thing."

"Really?" Andrew shyly asked, picking up a notepad of the dragon queen paper and some matching envelopes.

Tristan nodded and watched as his precious omega continued to scan the rest of the display with bright eyes. "Indeed. You're letting your cubs know that you're there for them, that you love them and that one day you will see them in person without any fears. They really adore it and they want to meet you one day too."

Having tensed up a little at those words, Andrew felt as though he was about to bolt out of the door before Tristan once again pressed a kiss to his neck and immediately he calmed down. It was still a very strange sensation to feel himself relaxed because his alpha was so close, but he supposed at some point he'd get used to it. Mentally he scolded himself for not really talking to other omegas about how it was with their alphas but then figured that realistically he hadn't been ready for those sorts of discussions. There were a lot of things that he still wasn't ready for, and he still did not quite understand how he could be so open with Tristan. He pushed aside those thoughts for now however and sighed. "It was just supposed to be a thing on their birthday and for Christmas but... hey! What are you doing?"

Whilst Andrew had been lost in his thoughts, Tristan had picked up another pack of paper along with matching envelopes and a couple of pens that matched with the male version of the Gingerbread Dragon. He seemed to be debating about some stickers that came with the set as well and was even holding onto a dragon-themed pencil case without apparently noticing that he had picked it up. Blinking, the alpha looked up at the omega and smiled. "Well it'd make sense for the cubs' daddy to start sending them messages since he's come back to protect and love their mother, wouldn't it?"

"No, that would be-!" started Andrew, who immediately got the wrong end of the stick as his already rather overstimulated mind jumped to the worst case scenario.

Tristan caught hold of Andrew's arm and gave him a gentle tug down into his space, releasing a small, concentrated blast of his tea tree scent to clear the omega's head just a little. "I meant me, Andrew, no one else. My uncle may have raised them, but you are their mother and I will gladly be their father beside you. I've already met them, Alban signed Daddy towards me and called me by that name... no one else. Me and you, Mummy and Daddy Dragon, okay?"

There was a long pause, until Andrew realised that there were tears of joy slipping down from his eyes. His heart swelled and he found himself turning to fully embrace Tristan, constantly chanting the same two words over and over again as he hid his face in the crook of the other's neck. "Thank you," he said, "thank you, thank you, thank you!"

Smiling as he held the taller omega to his chest, waving his hands in dismissal towards a curious shop assistant, Tristan gently guided Andrew to a seat that was brought across and allowed the omega to just curl up into his lap as if he were a tiny cub. They settled like that against one another, Tristan putting the shopping items in a little basket and started to hum in order to calm the omega further.

After a while, he placed a gentle kiss onto the side of Andrew's head. "Please tell me that you honestly didn't think that I would push you aside because you had those precious little cubs?"

A series of silent nods was his reply as the omega could barely make a sound out of his throat.

Tristan managed to tilt Andrew's head enough so that he could place a little kiss onto the others soft lips before lightly nipping at his nose. "Oh, baby, you're letting those nasty, little gremlins try to rule you again, aren't you?"

Andrew nodded and swallowed a little excess phlegm in his throat. "I'm sorry for them…"

"It's fine, my little one," Tristan replied and kissed his nose again. "Now, are we going to stay here, as a crying mess in the middle of the shop for the rest of the afternoon or should we pay up, go home and snuggle on the couch?"

A playful glare came his way and Tristan giggled. "Well okay, go and be sensible at your house then. I haven't caught up with your mother yet and she'll kick my tail if I don't. Plus, I want to annoy Daniel a little by proving that I am yours forever."

"You do know he's stopped doing that, right?" Andrew said, accepting another handkerchief from Tristan before furrowing his brow. "How many of these do you have?"

"On me?" Tristan did a mental little head count. "Three. I've got like six others at home."

Raising an eyebrow, Andrew let out a little bit of a giggle before hugging back into Tristan. "Thank you."

"Is that all you're going to say for the rest of the day?" Tristan smiled before getting back up onto his feet and helping Andrew to stand. Tristan leaned forward to give Andrew a little nuzzle on his nose and lightly pinch at his cheeks. "Come on, Mummy Dragon. Let's get these bought and then we can get you home before I make you cry anymore today."

"It's really not your fault," Andrew whispered, looking down at the floor again. "It's me who's the broken one."

"And I'll be the one who'll help fix you," Tristan replied, squeezing the other's hand tightly in reassurance before passing the basket over to the cashier to make their purchases.

A little giggle made his black ears twitch and he looked towards his mate with a raised eyebrow. Andrew continued to giggle before shaking his head. "How many pens did you buy?"

"Huh?" Looking at the bag which the cashier had filled and the price that was clearly displayed on the till, a bright red flush crossed Tristan's face as he realised that he had picked up at least twenty of the pens. For a second he panicked but then he grinned, "Well, the boys need pens for school work, right? So, Daddy Dragon can send them some because he owes them a lot of presents."

Smiling at that thought, Andrew shook his head and contained the squeal of adoration that wanted to desperately escape his lips. Instead he just happily linked his hand back with Tristan's as they exited the shop and blatantly ignored the coos coming from the shop assistants. They headed down the familiar roads in a comfortable silence and headed to collect Tristan's car, the alpha saying that the bookshop could wait. He really shouldn't add anything more to his to-be-read pile and he could behave and wait for another day. Andrew did not believe him at all, but was happy to indulge him a little.

As they drove through the streets, Andrew curled up in the passenger seat and nodded off quickly but Tristan was only more enamoured, as it meant that his omega felt secure enough to be in a vulnerable state of sleep around him. His inner alpha was preening with the knowledge, as well as standing proudly and protectively by Andrew's wolf to prove that he was the best one to protect him and no one was going to come anywhere near his lovely omega anytime soon. Tristan would make sure to take him home, get him tucked up in bed and then chat to Andrew's mother until either it got too late or Andrew woke up. It would be nice to catch up with Timothea, as it had been a long time and there was lots that needed to be talked about.

They drove in silence for a while, until a phone call pinged up on the hands free system. It was a call from Viola, which was unusual and made Tristan answer it immediately. "Hello, Vi? What's up?"

There was a pause. "Are you with Andrew?"

"Yes, he's asleep in the car with me," Tristan replied, detecting notes of panic in the other's voice. "What's wrong?"

Viola sighed long and hard before saying that she was moving from wherever she was. The alpha got nervous from that and spotted a place to safely pull over as he got the feeling that driving right now may not be a good idea. Andrew stirred in question and Tristan petted him gently.

Finally, after an agonizing thirty seconds, Viola came back on the line. "I'm sorry to call you but Mam and Dad are at work, Daniel's already on his way to come and collect the other two and I just didn't know who else to call."

"Wait? What's wrong with the cubs?" Tristan asked, feeling his stomach churning and noted that Andrew had become alert.

"It's Alban..." Viola said, her voice sounding strained and filled with tears which made a million and one thoughts race through Tristan's mind.

"What about Alban?" Tristan prompted, practically hearing Andrew scrabbling to get closer to the phone call even though he was as close as he could be right now. Tristan gently took hold of his omega's hand, giving him a squeeze to show that he was there with him and that they were in this together.

"I had to take him to hospital straight after his wushu practice today..." Viola started, her voice hiccupping with tears.

"What? Why?"

"Is he okay?"

"What happened?"

"Did someone attack him?"

"Whoa, stop with the questions," Viola snapped before letting out a sigh. "I don't know how to tell you this..."

"What?" both Tristan and Andrew asked at the same time.

"He's in heat."

To Be Continued

Sarah was diagnosed with dyslexia aged 10 and turned it into an passion for writing and was first published in 2016. She currently works in the outdoors during the day and writes in the evening and weekends, in south east England.